Trial 23

Harold Kish

Other stories from Lantern House:

Sugar Skin
Carnivores
Blackwood Manor
Witch Bones

Lantern House Publishing

This is a work of fiction. Names, characters, places, events, and incidents are either products of the author's imagination or are used fictitiously.

This book is the intellectual property of Mr. Harold Kish

Published by Lantern House Publishing, Nanaimo, B.C

https://www.lanternhousepublishing.com

Edited by Nicholas Wilson.

ISBN: 978-1-9991734-0-1

Trial 23

Harold Kish

The date is October 23rd, year unknown.

This marks my first entry in the notebook Doctor Windhelm gave me earlier today. He has instructed me to write down everything about my life here at Wentworth Psychiatric hospital, and to do so in as much detail as possible. That includes eating, sleeping, and whatever else I might do in this nut house. I don't remember having a diary before, but then again, I don't remember anything beyond waking up this morning.

At least I'll have something to do in my depressing cell, unless I decide to stab my eyes out with this pen.

First thing's first. My quarters are miserable. The good doctor has placed me inside a white cube. Four white walls and a white roof. Even the floor is white. The walls are so godlessly pale that I can see a muddled reflection of myself when I look closely, though my features are heavily distorted. I assume I'm handsome. They're even kind of soft, these walls. I could probably bang my head off them for hours without drawing blood. I might just do that. A little speckle of red would really liven the place up a bit.

Then there's my bed, lifeless, bland, miserable. It's a hunk of plastic stuck to the wall. It looks like an upside-down bathtub, solid so I can't crawl underneath it and gnaw my fingers off, or masturbate while I howl like an ape, or whatever people do in these types of asylums. I'm new. I can't say for certain.

Trial 23

It has a mattress on it. Hard, thin, uncomfortable…white.

The shining jewels of my inhuman prison are the sink and the toilet. Just fantastic. The tap gives me cold water and the toilet has no seat or lid or tank. It's like an airplane toilet, only I have to squat to shit. I might as well be in the forest. Fucking savage. At least the water is in ample supply. If I get too crazy and start painting the walls with my own feces, I can wash my hands after. So, that's something to look forward to.

There is an air grate above my head that won't shut up. It keeps making a droning sound, buzzing and buzzing like the good doctor is pumping chemicals into my room. If I'm not already wacked, I will be soon.

I almost forgot about the door. It's white. It has no window or handle. Chances of escape are pretty slim. It has a peephole for looking in but not for looking out. It is a bit creepy. Even creepier is the Plexiglass box in the upper corner of my room and its blinking red light. Are you watching me, Dr.? Am I pretty?

That's it for my cell. The place is drab and boring. If I don't kill myself, I will likely die of boredom. Either that or my brain will fry under the phosphorescent light bulbs. It's like a flash grenade went off in here but the light won't go away. It's blinding, unrelenting. I'm sure it will soon drive me mad.

I'll start at the beginning. It was several hours ago that I blinked into existence on this very mattress. I was groggy, confused. The obnoxious lighting burned my eyes. My initial thought was that I had died and was in a bright white hell. Maybe hell is better than here.

My second thought was not much of a thought, more of a panic. I lay in bed opening and closing my eyes, squirming and groaning, trying to place myself. Then I realized I couldn't. I was in an unfamiliar place and could not remember a damn thing. Not one. I rummaged through the chambers of my mind and came up empty. My memory bank was hollow, all the drives wiped clean.

I shot up like a coma patient jolted alive in their hospital bed, white sheet tucked beneath my legs. And then I thought, okay, I'm in a hospital, I've been injured, let's check out these legs of mine.

I prodded myself in the thighs, pinched my knees, and felt my junk. All still there, all with feeling, nothing damaged. A-Okay. Next, I lifted my white shirt and looked for wounds, finding none, just the bony ribs and thin, sickly pale flesh of a sick man in the hospital. Maybe, I thought, I was diseased. My head certainly hurt. My heart was palpitating so erratically I could feel the blood throb in my toes. And I was deathly thirsty. I needed water, and that was when I spotted the sink. I tried to go to it.

But standing was harder than anticipated. I swung my legs out and placed my feet on the floor, and it felt like a dozen wasps stung the soles of my feet. My nerves flared and I launched myself upwards and immediately fell. My legs were jelly and gave out like a pair of floppy noodles.

My knees hit the floor first. It felt like the bones burst into fragments. I cried out and flopped onto my face, nearly in tears. And now I'm laying on the floor in terrible agony. Helpless, feeling like a senior in an informercial who's fallen and can't get up.

I had to wriggle my way to the sink like a worm. A goddamn worm. My body was so weak, hands numb and tingly like they had been asleep for days. It was a miracle I made it to the sink. I managed to haul myself up like a cripple without his wheelchair and stick my mouth beneath the spout, turn the knob. And blessed be the water that gushed into my mouth! It was amazing. The water moistened my parched lips and satisfied my intense thirst. I let it splash over my face and soak my shirt. I must have guzzled thirty liters of cold water before I shut off the knob and collapsed, propped my back against the wall and stretched out my legs.

I sat there panting for a long time, eyes burning beneath the spotlights on the ceiling. I did not have a proper thought in my head. There was nothing I could remember, not my name, not my age, not a single aspect of my life. All I knew was the brightness seemed an element of the air itself, unyieldingly bright. I eventually crawled back to my bed and hid beneath the sheet.

I soon fell asleep, lulled unconscious by the soothing drone of the air duct above my bed.

I woke once after my initial resurrection in need of water. My legs worked a bit better and I got up to drink, then crawled back in bed and fell asleep. A second and third time followed, always thirsty.

When I got up the fourth time, it was to piss out all the water I had been guzzling. But then I was wide awake. I flushed my urine down the drain and sat on the edge of my bed, honestly afraid for my wellbeing. I had no identity that I could remember, no clue where I was, and no idea of the time. I was trapped in a timeless limbo, a bright purgatory where even myself had deserted me. Not to mention, I was starting to wonder what kind of hospitals have white rooms with no door handles.

Now hours are flying by, or maybe minutes. It was hard to tell. I paced my cell trying to get my legs to work properly. I lay in bed and stared at the ceiling, trying to remember anything at all. I drank more water. I peed a few more times. I waved frantically at the camera in the upper corner of my room. I screamed at it. I called it a whore. I showed it my bare ass.

Eventually, I tired. Endless seconds mounted over endless seconds and I lay flat on the cold floor, quite certain I was dead and in Hell, and that the timeless limbo was my eternal punishment.

Then people came. I still don't know their names. I call them Mr. Strong and Mr. Clean.

They loomed in my doorway like a pair of disgruntled eunuchs, the fucking eggheads staring at me with their dead, soulless eyes. I was still laying on the floor and I looked like an idiot. Maybe I should have gotten up, but instead I lay there and gawked at the bald buffoons in my doorway. I didn't know what to do. If I was indeed in Hell, these flinty-eyed primates made suitable caretakers.

Mr. Clean was tall. Mr. Strong was wide. They wore white dress shirts tucked into white khakis, smooth black belts. They had their shirts buttoned so tightly their necks bulged from their collars and they looked like muscular turtles. They were utterly hairless. They stank like cigarette smoke.

Mr. Strong told me to get up. "He wants to see you," he said.

I got up, a little nervous to meet the Devil.

Mr. Strong gestured me to follow him and his partner into the hallway, these two bullies. I could tell they were cruel. They had the look. It was unmistakable. Mr. Strong I could see stealing my lunch money and setting cats' tails on fire, growing into the stout, grumpy man I saw before me.

Mr. Clean was undeniably sinister. Tall and lanky, skeletal in the face. All he was missing was the trench coat. Fucking flasher. I could see the beak-nosed freak of a man masturbating in the woman's section of a department store or jacking off outside some poor girl's window, looking like a monster in the rain and the darkness.

Trial 23

"Who wants to see me?" I asked.

"The doctor," Mr. Strong said. He had the voice of a hog, all nasally.

"Alright."

A doctor felt more realistic than Satan. I guessed I was in a hospital. My gut told me exactly what kind. The white walls, the stern orderlies, the muffled screams I heard now that my door was open. A loony bin. That was it. I had woken up in a goddamn loony bin without my mind. I guessed that meant I was crazy.

I followed the glabrous eggheads into the hallway, seeing the plaque on my door as Mr. Clean swung it shut and locked it. The plaque said 244. It gave me chills to think there were 243 other nameless animals locked up in claustrophobic boxes like mine, squirming in perpetual brightness. It made me think of clones. I suddenly felt displaced, picturing 243 versions of myself waking up in cramped cells.

I could not tell how many doors were in the hallway. They looked to be infinite, like standing between two mirrors. To my right was an endless number of sealed white doors, a runway of dirty tiles that led to nothing. Light bulbs dangled from thin wires on the cracked plaster ceiling. Some were on but most were not, some flickered a dingy yellow aura. I could hear chatter from down the way, the sound of many muffled voices. Some of them were screaming. Some were arguing with themselves. Fucking wackjobs.

I stared down the dreary passage of locked chambers to where it faded and grew fuzzy and ultimately black as a cave's mouth. A sense that I was forlorn washed over me. I wondered how long I had been amongst the muffled voices. I thought, am I a long-term resident in this hall of the despondent?

Mr. Strong's fat hand nudged me to the left and we started down the hall. He said, "Hurry, he's waiting."

Down the hall we stopped at a metal fence, an old fashion prison gate with a thick mesh door and a padlock. Mr. Clean removed an archaic keyring with dozens of keys from his pocket, cycled through them and stuffed a bony skeleton key into the lock. The gate clicked open and we exited the depression of the hallway.

We passed a cafeteria, empty but for chairs and tables. There were rows of windows against the back wall trapped behind metal cages. The windows were streaked with rain and I could hear the faint pitter-patter of rain against tin as I walked by. I supposed it was raining outside. It was strange not knowing what month, what season, what year it was.

There came another gate and another key, an intersection without signage, four identical halls without end like we were at the nexus of some infinite and unpopulated office building. We went straight through the crossroads and happened by office doors with brass placards and names written on them. No one spoke during our walk. There was no sound from behind any of the closed doors. All I could hear was the dry wheezing of the mouth-breather, Mr. Strong, behind me. I had known him ten minutes and I already wanted to cram a dirty sock in his mouth and suffocate him.

They stopped me in front of a door with the name, Dr. Windhelm, etched in black on the placard. Mr. Clean knocked once and a voice from within invited us to enter.

The aroma was old books, dusty curtains and stale cigar smoke, a sealed library of parchment and scrolls fumigated by the billows of smoldering Havana tobacco. There were mahogany desks and tables, the leather sofa of an over-paid psychiatrist, globes and busy surfaces, university diplomas hung from panel walls. A window streaked with rain. Medical volumes on an oak shelf, row upon row in alphanumerical order. The odds and ends, trinkets and tokens, of a man's long and eccentric life. A carpet as red as Christ's blood covered the floor, something found in the den of a Persian prince.

Dr. Windhelm sat behind his desk, cluttered with pens and papers, stamps and staplers. There was an ashtray filled to the brim with brown cigar butts, moist and wilting. The man looked like an owl in a nest, I thought. His eyes were hidden behind circular spectacles, shaded a light tinge of black. His features were masked by a wispy cloud of white smoke. The stogie clenched between his teeth was half inhaled. Ash clung to it like a grey tower about to crumble.

"Leave," he said, his voice grizzled in a frightening way. Dr. Windhelm had the look of a man who burned jungle villages to the ground and raped indigenous women; a primitive and bearded savage in a knit sweater.

Mr. Strong and Mr. Clean fucked off and left me alone with the good doctor. I was a little intimidated. He exuded incredible power, an unsettling amount of indifference. There was something criminal about his nature.

"Sit," he told me, and gestured to one of the chairs at his desk.

I sat, squirmed a bit while the doctor puffed on his cigar and stroked his bushy beard. He was studying me. I felt like a test subject. When he grinned, he showed off the big chunks of teeth in his mouth. He sucked one final huff of tobacco. The cherry glowed and smoke swelled in his open mouth like there was a fire in his lungs. I clutched the armrests tightly as Dr. Windhelm exhaled smoke from his nose, ears, mouth, then snuffed out the corona in his ornamental ashtray. The guy was giving me a panic attack. I had been delivered from my stark prison into the lair of a smoky beast.

"How do you feel?" he asked.

"Fine."

"Fine?" Dr. Windhelm scoffed. "Surely you cannot feel fine. Surely you must feel small and overwhelmed, confused and disoriented, curious and out of depth."

"I am a little confused," I said. It felt like Dr. Windhelm wanted me to be confused, to be a frightened, to be a sniveling thing powerless before him. "I can't remember my name. I don't know where I am. I guess this is a hospital."

"The very best hospital in the country," Windhelm said, boastful and narcissistic. "You are in Wentworth Psychiatric Hospital, dear boy. You are in my hospital. It is the 23rd of October and you have been dormant in a coma for some time. You have been stricken with amnesia."

That sounded right. It felt like I had amnesia.

I asked, "Do you know who I am?"

"No. You are patient number 7098. We call you John. You were thrown from a taxi as it rolled off the West Bridge and into McGuire Lake. The driver was killed. You were found without a wallet. You were in general admission at St. Clemency General Hospital for weeks, disoriented and unaware, very clearly stricken by amnesia. When no family came to claim you, the hospital sent you here, where you slipped in and out of a coma for the last month."

"Why?" I did not understand. "Why would they send me to a nuthouse?"

Dr. Windhelm crinkled his nose and pursed his lips. "This is not a nuthouse, Mr. John Doe. This is a rehabilitation center for people suffering from curable afflictions of the mind. We help lost souls recover themselves, reaffirm their grasps on reality and seize control of their lives. We do this using therapy and other mind-altering procedures. Those whom we cannot help, we ease through what remains of their frail and broken existences."

"Sounds like a nuthouse to me," I said. "Will you heal my amnesia?"

Windhelm laughed, chuckled heartily and the cigar smoke floating around his head laughed with him, the doctor tittering madly inside a gaseous black cloud. "I will try, dear boy. I will try. Cases like yours are often irreversible. Yet we have ways to coax your memories back."

He sounded villainous. I envisioned a long metal hook being slipped up my nose, Dr. Windhelm chewing on his stogie while he scooped out pieces of my brain. And now my anxiety was in full swing. I chewed my lip, terrified of the doctor's spectacles gleaming like black ice. They looked like his eyes, like he had huge black eyes and was laughing at me.

"What I want you to do is begin a journal," he said. "Write down everything you do here at Wentworth, your activities throughout the day, your thoughts, any memories that jangle loose. This is how we will start. Perhaps by writing down your feelings, something from your past will be unearthed."

"Okay," I said. I was shaking. A panic attack bore down on me and I looked around at the strange ornaments and idols displayed throughout Windhelm's vapory office. They came alive. The statue of an elephant shot me a cruel wink and its trunk shook violently. A set of wooden monkeys, one covering its mouth, the other its eyes, and the third its ears, removed their hands, clapped and screeched. A globe on the doctor's desk started spinning. The painting of an eagle clanked its beak and clawed at the fish it had caught, guts and tiny bones splashing over the majestic bird's feathers.

"Thankfully," Windhelm said, "amnesia does not affect the general workings of the mind. It only blockades personal memories. Everyday things will still make sense to you, language, culture, eating, mechanical memories. Only your inner self is gone, buried somewhere in the catacombs of your mind. We must be clever if we wish to draw him out."

My skin was vibrating. The walls were closing in. "Okay," I said. Strange as it was, I wanted to get the hell out of Windhelm's office and back to my cell before I broke down and cried. I was in a fully-fledged hysteria. My heart palpitated and my palms were sweaty. I was a nameless, brainless outcast stuck in a mental hospital, a mad scientist yammering at me through a stale cloud of cigar smoke. Perhaps it was the sensation of nothingness that had me panicked, the notion that I was an empty husk of man, imprisoned without hope.

Windhelm said, "You are not a prisoner, per se. You were not committed here in the classic sense of the word. Yet all the same, we cannot allow a man without an identity to wander the streets. In the eyes of the law, you are a danger to yourself and to others. We prefer to think of you as our guest, not as our detainee. Though truthfully, you are not permitted to leave until we discover who you are."

"Okay." There was nothing more I could say. I trembled, totally unhinged. The doctor had me spooked. I had myself spooked. A thousand questions fizzled on my tongue, but I was too skittish to ask any of them. Windhelm handed me a notebook and a few pens. I kept thinking how this had happened before. I kept thinking how wrong this was, like I had somewhere else I needed to be.

"Do not stab yourself in the eyes," he told me. "The pens are only for writing."

Trial 23

I nodded, stuffed the pens in my pocket and clutched the notebook to my chest. "I can go now?" I couldn't stand being in the room with the doctor, burly old fuck behind his desk. The way he looked at me was predatory and added to my irrational fear. I hated the things he was telling me, that I was the victim of a car accident, my mind in tatters and me trapped in the haunted corridors of an insane asylum. How does that even happen? And to whom!

"Yes, you may." Windhelm called for the orderlies and they came into the room, the bald creeps with their glassy eyes. "I understand this is scary," the doctor said. He must have seen how I shivered in fear. "Try to remain calm. Focus on discovering yourself. Write down your experiences. Get comfortable. Wentworth is your home now. We will take care of you like you're one of our own."

That made it worse. Take care of me like one of their own? Like I was an unstable psychotic? I gave Windhelm a look, my face pinched. "What if I don't remember?"

"We will cross that bridge when we get to it," he said. "For now, go and rest. It is not an easy thing to wake from a coma. Your mind is strained. Things may appear strange for the next few days."

Strange was a fucking understatement. Things appeared totally fucked. I let Mr. Strong and Mr. Clean bring me to my cell and I sat down on my bed and stared at the wall. After a while, a nurse brought me food. When I finished eating the disgusting hospital slop, I started to write.

And now here I am, still wondering how they can keep me locked up if I have not committed a crime. Do I not have rights? Am I not a person? If I never recall who I am, then what? Am I forsaken here forever, a prisoner in this hellish cubicle? No matter what Windhelm said, I am undoubtedly a prisoner.

The Journal of Dr. W. Windhelm. Dated 23rd of October, the year 2010.

My patient awoke today. Boris came to my office to tell me. Boris said John was waving at the camera, showing the camera his bare ass. A lot of energy for a man fresh out of a coma. Good. He is going to need it.

    We have a lot of work to do if John is to regain his memories and make it through the trials. It will not be fun for him. I have waited an eternity for another amnesiac, having to subject the other unfortunate degenerates here in my hospital to the procedure in the meantime. They fared less than well. Indeed it has been rather tragic. The dungeons are nearly full, and I am sure Doctor Mandalay is beginning to falter under the weight of the incinerator.

    Yet finally, John washed onto the doorstep of my hospital. A pure amnesiac. The most influential of patients. Yes, I had to steal him from St. Clemency General Hospital. He did not really wash up on my doorstep. Yet he is mine now. Mine and awake.

Trial 23

    The others before John were pitiful cases. Patient 7047 ended in suicide. The three before her suffered incurable psychotic breakdowns, complete forfeitures of self. I remember still how they raved, the horrible screams like the wails of tortured apes, as if I were zookeeper in some twisted circus. A shame none survived the trials; at least not in any practical sense of the word.

    Yet where the other patients were lost so easily to the nightmare abyss, I have high hopes that John will overcome. We met just now in my office. He was confused and afraid but controlled himself well. I already believe him to have more potential than the previous amnesiacs, the idiots who fell prey to the dark void of madness. John did exhibit symptoms of anxiety and paranoia. His pupils were dilated and he appeared to be on the verge of hysteria. Yet these afflictions work to make his mind malleable. They make him controllable. So long as John does not descend into delusional anarchy, his unbalanced brain will make him highly susceptible to the treatment.

    Ah, the treatment. We have learned a great deal from past trials. Bad science and weak minds resulted in the failures of the other patients. Yet Doctor Mandalay and I have created a new procedure, and now we have John Doe as our subject. He has

just the right amount of aloof
insanity to make it work.

    Though even if he did not, I
have faith in my science. Mandalay
and I have perfected the treatment.
My benefactors will be quite pleased,
while the dullards over at the
Institute will be in awe over what I
have accomplished, a true revelation
of science. When John comes through
alive and regains his memories, I
will have changed the face of science
and the human mind forever. And if he
goes insane, becomes a drooling doll
of a man, still my investors will be
pleased.

    Doctor Mandalay will begin the
procedure tomorrow. She will give
John a check-up first thing in the
morning, the usual tests. She is a
squeamish woman, but she will see it
through. Ten years we have worked
together and still I wonder about
that woman's commitment. Yet she will
see it through for her own sake.

    I await tomorrow night to read
John's journal, to see the first step
in his journey. I only hope he is
articulate in his telling.

Trial 23

The date is October 24th, year still unknown.

I had hoped to wake this morning with the memories of my past back where they belong.

They weren't. I remember nothing of my life before yesterday. Where do I live? What kind of job do I have? Is there a cat in my house, dead because no one's there to feed it and now it's a bloated corpse being picked apart by flies? What if I have a baby? What if there's an infant's rotted body in a crib somewhere? It makes me nauseous to think about.

Best to focus on other things, like the nightmare of today. What a hellish ride.

I woke as the depressed owner of a void in my brain and a hollow nothingness in my soul, a walking ghost. I awoke to the thugs with their beady eyes and polished skulls glaring at me in my doorway. Mr. Strong, the human hippopotamus. And his friend, Mr. Clean, the beaky scarecrow.

My grim caretakers gestured me into the hallway. I went first to the sink for a gulp of water and took a nice long piss, the sound of my urine splashing in the drain while the eggheads watched me. Only then did I wash my hands and follow them into the corridor.

I immediately heard the wails of the damned stifled behind the walls of their prisons. All 243 psychotic inmates babbling and screaming in a manic discord. I was glad when Mr. Strong and Mr. Clean shoved me in the other direction, away from the dim mineshaft of sealed doors and flickering lightbulbs, the wretched hall of the accursed.

Again, we passed the metal gate and the cafeteria and arrived at the crossroads. We took a right this time. They brought me down an empty hallway and I found myself wondering again where the staff were. How could Wentworth be so big yet so vacant?

The dummies stopped at an open door. The placard read, M. Mandalay.

"He's here," Mr. Clean said. And a woman's voice told him, "Okay, you can leave him and go."

Mr. Clean gave me a distrusting look, sneering down his beak at me. "Behave," he said, as if I would do something stupid and commit myself to Wentworth for any longer than necessary. Then he shoved me into the room and closed the door.

It was bright like my cell. Medical instruments glowed white, tall silver stands with swivel heads shining like miniature lighthouses. There were foldable spotlights fixed to the ceiling. It looked like a surgical room. Everything was white and shining, metal trays with stainless tools, an M.R.I machine with its circular portal like the entrance to a spaceship's escape pod.

Doctor Mandalay sat at a desk in the corner beside a large console with buttons and a dark screen. Her hair was knotted in a bun. She wore square geeky glasses and had a nervous smile, blinked at me with timid blue eyes. "Welcome," she said.

"Hello."

"My name is Margaret. Margaret Mandalay. Or Doctor Mandalay, if you prefer. Some of the patients call me Dr. M. You can call me whatever you want."

"Okay." I didn't much care what to call her. I asked, "Why am I here?"

"Dr. Windhelm wants to do a complete physical on you. It's typical check-up stuff. You'll be out of here

Trial 23

in a jiffy."

"And back in my cell?" I'd have rather sat with Mandalay than stared at the white walls of my prison. The woman was a mouse, nervous and twitchy, but she was better company than my empty thoughts.

"Yes." She squirmed awkwardly in her seat. "I'm sorry. It sucks, I know. Hopefully we can get your memories back soon. Let's start with the simple stuff."

Mandalay was petite, cute in a helpless sort of way. She had me cough, listened to my lungs and my heart. She took my blood-pressure and checked my reflexes. She gave me some white pills and said they were to help alleviate my stress. Then she looked in my ears, my nose, shone a flashlight in my eyes. She told me, "Try not to let the orderlies bother you. Doctor Windhelm hired them because they do what he says, heartless monsters. Not sure where he found them, but they are useful for some of our more... unruly guests."

I bet they were. I thought of the 243 wackos down the hall from me, 243 victims for Mr. Strong and Mr. Clean to torment. It was unsettling to think two men so clearly evil had nearly 300 dementia-stricken people at their disposal. I was sure they did at least a little torturing. I was sure they had fun discipling the more... unruly guests.

Doctor Mandalay was feeling my lymph nodes. Her hands were cold and clammy. Still, the touch of a woman had me slipping into a nervous jitter. It was Windhelm's office all over again. My jaws locked and my mouth went dry. She was saying something... "You're a very special case, John. It's rare that we have someone with us who doesn't belong, someone who has no mental disorders." All I could focus on was her squirrely face, her tiny mouth moving. She looked like a goldfish.

"It's why we need to get your memories back sooner than later. I don't want you to be here any longer than necessary." She sounded earnest enough. I believed her. And I liked her more than the three other people I had met. She struck me as honest, caring, having a heart. I was sweating so badly that when Dr. Mandalay finished feeling my throat, she had to wipe her hands on her pants.

"Everything checks out," she said. "You're in good shape, asides from the atrophy caused by your coma. But that will heal."

"Good," I said, "I feel weak." I felt dizzy, too, overwhelmed for no reason. My right leg would not stop bouncing.

She said, "The weakness will pass."

Doctor Mandalay went to her desk and booted up her computer monitor. "I want to put you through the M.R.I machine to scan your brain," she said. "Maybe we can find a clue about what caused your amnesia."

"Okay." I looked at the machine, the giant kitchen appliance in Doctor Mandalay's office. It appeared harmless enough, kind of futuristic. The Dr. pushed some buttons and a long bed was ejected slowly from its mouth. She invited me to lay on it. My irrational anxiety had my hands tingling.

"It's going to get very noisy," she said. Dr. Mandalay pushed a button and my bed began to slide into the machine. It felt like I was being cremated, like I was sliding into a furnace in the basement of a charnel house. The thought had me panicked. I could feel pricks on my back like the tips of flames. It was bright and I shut my eyes, tried to calm my nerves. Why the hell did this keep happening to me, this unwarranted panic? Was I a schizophrenic in my past life?

Mandalay was fussing with the controls, babbling to herself. She said, "Here it comes," and a terrible buzz filled the metal tube. It was loud, boring through my

Trial 23

skull and into my brain. A banal whirr vibrated my bones. I started to hyperventilate. It felt like I was being rocketed into space. I squeezed my eyes tighter and focused on the buzz, let it take me until my body was one single vibration, my mind listless in dead space.

What happened next in Doctor Mandalay's office was nothing short of outrageous. The drone of the machine must have lulled me to sleep. It must have coaxed me into a dream. When my eyes opened, the machine was in the middle of powering down. The light flickered and the loud buzz turned into a dying squeal. The M.R.I chugged and knocked like it was out of gas. It made one final clunk and the lights cut out.

"Mandalay?"

No one answered. It was dark and hushed. I bent my neck and looked down the length of my tube, seeing nothing but blackness. Then a door creaked open and a wide beam of light spilled in. A woman entered, walked to the kitchen sink and gripped its basin, hung her head sadly. All I could see was her slouched back. Then she started to cry softly.

"Hey," I said. "Hey, you, let me out of this thing."

She didn't hear me.

I tried to shimmy out of the cylinder but a gate swung down from the outside and sealed off the tube with a loud clank. It looked like a rusted sewer grate at the end of a drainage pipe, me trapped inside. I kicked at the bars to no avail. They were solid. I could do nothing but watch through the bars.

Moonlight drifted through the window above the sink where the woman still loitered sadly. Dirty dishes were stacked on the countertop. The kitchen table had bottles of ketchup and mayonnaise on it. The woman must have just finished dinner and was at the sink to clean up, yet all she did was sob. She was eerie, ghoulish in the dimly lit kitchen.

The ceiling fan groaned to life and its bulb flickered, casting gloomy radiance into the kitchen, a sort of yellow film over the shadows. Each time a blade passed the dying bulb the entire room eclipsed. I could hear the steady *swoosh... swoosh... swoosh* of every rotation as though a great vulture beat its wings.

Voices seeped through the open door. Someone was watching tv, a game show, contestants guessing the price of a new cutlery set. Fifty dollars, fifty-one, seventy-two. A man shouted at the television, "Five-four dollars."

And the gameshow host said, "89.99."

A rumble of curses from the man. "Fuck your mother, skinny bitch." He burped. I heard a bottle smash.

The woman at the counter sobbed louder. She still gripped the basin, but now she was rocking back and forth as if about to dash her face through the window and thrash amongst the fragments, slice her throat on the glass and fill the sink with blood. She was totally unhinged. She rocked faster and faster, seeming to gain confidence, to inch closer to a brutal suicide. Her hair flailed, her shawl fluttering like a cape. I thought for sure she was about to crash through the glass.

Then she stopped, so suddenly I'm surprised she didn't fall over. The gameshow had finished and thundersome steps came booming towards the kitchen. The woman stared at the doorway. A fan blade hummed in front of the bulb and the kitchen froze like a black and white photo. I blinked once and everything changed. The kitchen was still frozen, but now something hideous loomed in the doorway.

Hard to describe such a monstrosity. It was almost a man, but not quite. Its bare chest was thick

Trial 23

with shaggy black hair like a fucking gorilla. It wore ripped jeans and had the feet of a wolf, sharp yellow nails. It had claws for hands and the face of a human; only, it was not real. The face was waxen and imperfect. Beady eyes shone through mushy skin, a soggy mask.

It, he, whatever the beast was, stepped into the kitchen and the woman flinched, cowered before it. "Please," she said, "please don't hurt me."

It opened its mouth and made a sound like a swarm of bees, regarding the frail woman with marble eyes, black in its doughy face. I could see where its mask ended in a loose flap of skin on its neck, where its hide began. Its true skin was black and crispy.

"No." She inched backwards. "Please don't. I can fix it. I swear I can fix it."

It made another buzzing sound, a hive of wasps in the fiend's throat. It sounded angry. Then it removed its belt and looped it around its clawed hand. The woman pleaded, "Please no," and raised her hands in defense. It pulled back and gave her a lashing. She shrieked as the belt snapped across her wrists, the smack of leather on skin like a gunshot.

"Oh god no!"

It hit her again. It slapped her across the face with its belt and she fell to her knees. The kitchen shuddered, grew dim and the bulb on the fan shattered. I could hear her scream, hear the lash of the belt. But it was dark. There was nothing to be seen. The beast's demonic laughter resounded inside my tube.

Licks of light came from an unknown source, spasming the world in flashes of brightness. I saw volcanic rock, a great plain of jagged stones and the woman cowering in moth-eaten rags, looking like a peasant in Hell. Her tormentor had shed its skin, its mask melted off and its scruffy hair fallen out. What remained was a hellion with a leather whip. HE was a demon with red eyes and black, scabrous flesh, pocked and glowing like a thing risen from a bubbling pit of fire.

In the blinking light he whipped her without mercy, the stony demon. I had to close my eyes against the violence. It was brutal and made me sick. I couldn't stand the woman's shrieks. When I dared to look again, they were back in the kitchen under the light of the spinning fan. But it was just a man. Just a man with a flabby chest and bare feet, a mean temper as he beat the woman half to death with his fists. He was no demon, no devil. He was just a man.

The fan spun in slow circles, *swoosh... swoosh... swoosh...* the beating of heavy wings. On the floor was the woman, contorted hideously in a pool of blood. She looked dead.

That was when the gate at the end of my tube broke off, clattered to the floor without me touching it. I immediately slithered out and into the kitchen, stood with the laminate cold beneath my feet. When I turned to see what sort of tunnel I had been trapped in, there was nothing there, just a patch of blackness like a void in space.

I approached the woman, stepped into her pool of blood and it oozed between my toes, warm and squishy black. I hunkered next to her. "Can you hear me?"

She didn't answer. Her breath was shallow and weak, hair matted to her open wounds. I peeled away bits of wet hair until I got a good look at her face, though it was not much of a face anymore, lumpy and bruised, cut and gashed, more blood than skin. "Are you alright?" I asked. "Can you hear me?"

I reached for her, thinking to shake the woman awake. She came alive before I could, snatched hold of my wrists and pulled me down into her blood, then

Trial 23

scuttled onto me with unbelievable speed like a goddamn goblin. She sat on my chest and dug her fingernails into my face. "What have you done?" Her eyelids were inflamed, the balls inside red and angry. "Why are you here?"

"It wasn't me." I squirmed, the woman frothing above me like a mad witch. "I did nothing."

"Why are you here?" Her voice came out raspy, as if her throat had been strangled. "You shouldn't be here. You don't belong. Why have you come?"

"I don't know what you're talking about," I said. She was terrifying, gnashing her broken teeth, spitting blood in my eyes.

"You don't remember?" She calmed slightly. There was something cordial in the way she inspected me. Her face was horribly beaten, bruised beyond recognition, yet there was something soft and caring behind the destruction. "You must remember," she said. "Remember or spend eternity in darkness. Is that what you want, to be lost to the abyss?"

"No." It came out a whimper.

"Then leave this place!" She opened her mouth and disconnected her lower jaw, the sound of cracked bone and torn sinew. Her tongue lagged out, long and black. It was as if she wanted to kiss me, but her mouth was full of chipped teeth. They sunk into my cheek and I screamed, blood flowing into mouth, down my neck. It was so warm. She dragged her teeth down my forehead like a rake and blood soaked into my eyes, a sensation of warmth washing over me.

I guess I pissed myself. That was the warm sensation I felt. I woke screaming inside the M.R.I machine, slapping the walls and crying out for help. My pants were soaked. I guess I pissed myself.

Doctor Mandalay heard my screaming and stopped the machine, ejected me out of it. I scrambled off the flat bed and scurried into the corner of the room, dropped and hugged my knees. I was panting, confused, out of place and out of mind. It had only been a dream, yet I remembered it vividly. It had felt real. I sat hunched with my knees against my chest and trembled. I still felt the woman's teeth in my face. I kept touching my cheek to see if it was bleeding.

"John, is everything alright?" Dr. Mandalay stooped in front of me. "What happened?"

"I had a dream," I told her, a little calmer with Mandalay's mousy face to look at, to keep me grounded. "I must have fallen asleep in your machine and had a nightmare. The buzz was hypnotic."

Mandalay looked doubtful. "I only turned the machine on for a second, John. You were inside it for less than three minutes before you started screaming." She scrunched her nose. "Did you…"

We both looked, my white hospital pants stained dark yellow. I reeked like piss.

"It was the nightmare," I said. I was so embarrassed. I wanted to curl in a ball and cry. "I'm sorry, I didn't mean to."

She gave me a pitiful look, like I was a dog that didn't know any better than to piss on the floor. "Oh, John, don't be sorry. You've just woken from a long coma with amnesia. Your mind is fragile. You need more time to heal. It's okay."

It didn't feel okay. I had walked into Dr. Mandalay's office a normal man who had forgotten who he was. Ten minutes later and I was another one of her wackjob patients, sniveling about nightmares and cowering in the corner with piss in my pants. What the fuck was that? A ten-second nightmare that felt more real than life? Was being in a mental hospital making me lose it? Maybe a runoff from the coma, a lingering dream state.

Trial 23

"I want to go back to my cell."

"Okay, John. Everything will be okay."

Mandalay helped me to my feet and guided me into a chair beside her desk. She dialed some numbers on her phone and asked for the orderlies to come get me. I had to sit there smelling like urine for ten minutes while we waited, Dr. Mandalay even more awkward than I was. She kept trying to make small talk. "Do you like dogs, John?"

"I can't remember."

"Of course not. Sorry, how rude of me."

Mr. Strong and Mr. Clean showed up and Dr. Mandalay told me to take care, that she would see me soon. She was sweet and it made me feel a little better about peeing my pants.

The bastard eggheads took me to my cell, snickering at me the whole way. I couldn't blame them. Not really. I waddled down the empty hallways with a big piss stain on my ass.

A nurse brought me a change of clothes and later I was escorted to the cafeteria to eat with the rest of the lunatics. What a bunch of sorry fucks. They rambled, argued, threw food, broke down and cried. It was like eating lunch with toddlers. Only, these were grown men in the depths of madness, rocking in their chairs, talking to shadows. They barked at me and jittered insanely. An old man got up on the table and showed me his wrinkled pecker, then was subdued by an orderly and hauled off screaming and pissing all over the place. I was glad when Mr. Clean escorted me back to my room.

It's bright in here. I hate it. Why will no one turn off the lights? I am sick of this place. I want to go home. Yet, do I even have a home to go back to? Is there a crummy apartment waiting for me beyond these walls? Do I have a family, friends, a woman who loves me? I cannot recall. Not a damn thing. My only memories are of the last 48 hours in Wentworth Hospital. The closest thing I have to a friend is the skittish Dr. Mandalay. My most vivid memory is of my nightmare in the M.R.I machine. I can still see the battered woman clear as day, her red eyes as she screamed at me to remember. If only it was that easy.

    The hour grows late. The fucking lights are still on. I want to sleep, yet I fear what will happen when I drift off. If I dream, will it be of horrors? If I shut my eyes, will I be transported to another realm of violence and brutality? I pray the answer is no. I just want some rest. Two days and I already hate this place.

Trial 23

Margaret's Journal: 10/24/10

Poor John. He's lost. Amnesia is a terrible curse. I can't imagine it, to hit my head so hard it erases the person I am. Although, perhaps for me it would be alright. I could start over, forget I ever came to Wentworth, forget ever meeting Dr. Windhelm, forget ever participating in these trials.

Poor John. What he must be going through. It's devastating to watch, to see him screaming in fright and losing control over his bladder, to see him tremble in the corner of my office, to see the fear in his eyes. I can't bear to watch another amnesiac go insane. I can't. It's too much. They would have been better off as new people, starting new lives. Anything would have been better than going mad, getting stuck in their own personalized nightmares. Poor 7047, jabbed a pen straight through her eye and into her brain.

If John begins to slip into madness, I think I'll pull him out. My heart can't take another loss. He's such a sweet man, an innocent man. It shames me to have stolen him from St. Clemency General Hospital. He would have been set free, assisted by the government to begin a new life. Now Windhelm's got him. He's already started the procedure to "enhance" John's mind. I saw the devastating results of it this morning.

But Windhelm's right. Amnesiacs are the best subjects, their minds scrubbed clean, able to be reconstructed more easily. I remember when we first started tinkering, trying to repair the shattered psyches of our more deranged patients. But there was nothing to build on. We had no way to check our procedure. They were already demented. The process only pushed them deeper into dementia. Some of them are still locked in the basement.

Windhelm thinks we've perfected it now, made the formula perfect through trial and error. He thinks John will be the confirmation of our ability to mold minds. It's an exciting thought. The applications are endless. To manifest a world within a mind, to allow people the freedom to walk through memories, to relive their pasts, to puzzle out their futures. It would be a new phase for the world, better than computer simulations or video games. Just think, to have control over one's dreams!

It's the inner workings that are a tad confusing, the science behind brain manipulation and imagination construction. It's why it took us so long to get this far. Not to mention, it's illegal what Windhelm and I are doing. We're practically giving drugs to children to see how they react, then tweaking the formula and giving them to different children. Poor John. He's just a mindless boy being force-fed drugs.

I won't let him die like the others. If after all these years we still fail to generate a malleable program within the mind, a means to contort reality and enhance brain power, I'll quit. I've had enough. The possibilities for good are what's made me stay, but I can't take the losses. I can't take how corrupted our attempts have become. I hope Windhelm's right. I hope this time we succeed.

October 25$^{th.}$ Day 3.

My cell was dark when I awoke in the night. A dreary red glow shone through the air vent above my bed, cast a shadow on my wall like the mouth of a furnace. Though I was more confused about the ceiling, it wasn't there. Blackness stretched upwards forever. I was in a box without a roof like a room at the bottom of the blackest part of the sea.

Sounds drifted through the vent above my bed, someone singing. I got on my tiptoes to peek through the thin bars of the grate. On the other side was a child's bedroom. Right there on the other side of my wall, a little girl sitting peacefully on the floor and singing quietly to herself. On her bedside table was one of those rotating lamps with animal shapes cut into its shade, throwing silhouettes of bears and tigers and monkeys on her wall. Yet the bulb in the lamp was red. The animals looked terribly evil as they circled the girl's room. Hungry, even.

The little girl was drawing with crayon. She had one clutched in her hand, working it like a wand over the page of a coloring book. More pages were spread around the child like a spattering of crime scene photos. The sheets were chalked heavily in red, crayon smeared over the outlines of happily smiling animals. The tune she hummed was pleasant. She sang as she worked, *"Dumh de de dumh. Do do do dee. Dee dee dee da. Dumh de de dumh."*

It was tranquil, a touch familiar. I could have

listened to her sing all night, her sweet voice. It was angelic. Something about the moon outside her window, the pale and bony trees, it was relaxing. And I liked the girl, her melody, her mouth screwed in an expression of dull satisfaction as she colored. It filled me with subtle happiness.

Then I smelt it, the burning, the scent of melted wax and charred feathers. I dug my fingers into the grate and squinted harder into the girl's room, seeing now that she gripped her crayon too tightly. Red wax oozed between her tiny fingers. She no longer worked the crayon like a wand but like a knife, stabbing at the page, carving it and tearing the paper with her crayon.

Her face turned ugly. Her eyebrows curved and she scowled, teeth sunk hard into her bottom lip. It was some form of madness. She was trying to erase the page with her crayon, blotting out the picture with a smear of red.

A tap from the window above her bed drew my attention. A raven had perched itself on the windowsill and stared at me with pearl white eyes, hungry, unnatural. I thought I could hear its thoughts, whispering evil desires in my head. The bird cawed, then dashed its beak against the glass, mocking me with its malignant animal stare.

The girl continued to hum as the bird tapped frantically on the window, smearing wax on her coloring book. The raven could have been a woodpecker for all its tapping, bashing away at the glass with its beak. The glass made ping sounds and cracked as the bird grew more and more frenzied, flapped its wings and sent surges of dark feathers to float off into the night.

Another black-winged rodent landed on the windowsill and began to hit the glass with its skull, both birds going berserk, leaping in the air and scratching

Trial 23

with their talons, ruffling their feathers and pecking the glass until it shattered in a hail of shards.

Still, the girl did not move. She continued to scribble even as ravens poured in through the window, clustered on her bed, landed on her carpet and began to peck at her legs. There were dozens of them. I screamed through the grate, "There are too many, get out!" But she hummed, face twisted in anger, stabbing the coloring book with her crayon.

The room erupted in a storm of black feathers. The birds tore out chunks of carpet, fluttered in front of the bookshelf and flung scraps of paper about the room. They clawed at the wallpaper. They landed on the girl's head, her shoulders, snatched tufts of her hair with their flinty beaks. Their squawking was the worst of it, loud and incessant. Yet underneath the squall of birds was the girl's song. She sang, *"Dumh de de dumh. Do do do dee. Dee dee dee da. Dumh de de dumh."*

Even as they thrashed about her head in a tumult circle, she sang. Even as they shredded her precious coloring book, she sang. Even as one of them snatched the crayon from her hand and snapped it in half, she sang. And she continued to sing as they swarmed her, tore slices of skin from her face, her little child arms, bit off her fingers and swallowed them.

Three dozen birds encapsulated the child, now invisible beneath the panic of their wings, her song dead, replaced by the wet and sloppy sounds of a feast as the birds ate her alive. They were a writhing mass, a cyclone of beaks and feathers all speckled with blood. And they began to morph. The swarm condensed and crunched itself into the shape of a person, an eight-foot man made of beaks and claws and feathers, birds mutated to form limbs and feet and hands. It was a hideous mess, all those ravens broken into place. Wings twitched along its shoulders and beaks clanked inside its legs, dozens of white blinking eyes displaced inside its malformed body.

    The thing squawked and flailed its arms, knocking the girl's lamp off the table and onto the carpet, onto some scraps of paper and feathers. The smell was immediate as they caught flame, the stench of burning wax and burning feathers. The agitated bird-monster opened the door and walked out of the room in a bluster of squawks and fidgety wings.

    I plugged my nose against the smell as smoke began to rise from the fire spreading across the carpet. I let myself down from the grate, feeling like I had just witnessed something terribly tragic.

Noxious smoke was wafting into my cell through the vent. I had to get out of there. I ran at the door, rammed it with my shoulder and the damn thing burst apart like rotten wood. I flew into the hallway on a plume of black smoke.

    To the right was nothing, the same void that had been above my room. It unnerved me. I felt that if I strayed into the nothingness, it would absorb my soul. The fear of it had me pivoting left and fleeing down the hall.

    I came to the little girl's room in a few short steps. Tendrils of smoke slithered from beneath her door. A sign was posted to it, a slice of paper with a name written in red crayon. I couldn't read it. The heat had melted the letters, made them runny.

    I kept on. The hallway was dingy and claustrophobic, wet shag carpet under my bare feet and peeling wallpaper. It stretched on forever in a neglected sort of gloom. On the walls were cracked picture frames and I stopped to inspect one, an old family photograph, boy and girl, mother and father, all huddled closely before the family sofa. Their faces were too small for me to see, smudged in the old photograph. They looked

Trial 23

happy enough.

Down the way I found another, the frame hung crooked on the wall. It was the same family in the same room, positioned a little differently. They looked away from each other as if in disgust.

Another few feet down the hall came another frame and another photo, same family but now distraught. The father's face had been singed out of the picture, his hands raised in fury. The children cowered, mother's face streaked with tears.

I understood a tale was being told, some tragic dissolution of a family. I rushed down the hall to the next photo, which showed the family in complete disorder. The little girl, the same one who had been picked apart by ravens, was sideways on the couch. The boy sat with his back against the sofa, face buried in his hands. The mother and father were at odds, locked in a desperate struggle. Again, the father's face was burnt out of the photo.

Moving along, I came upon the family's horrific conclusion. This picture had no frame, just a flimsy photograph nailed to the wall, the nail driven through the face of the father. What I saw in the picture made me despair, gasp and turn from it. Such senseless violence, such corruption, a shocking exhibition of barbarism. It turned my guts, had me standing in the silence of the long hallway trying to find some reason, some meaning in such cruelty. I was glad when the photo flamed and turned to ash, nothing but an old rusty nail stuck in the wall.

I took a deep breath and kept moving. There was a door a few feet ahead.

Like the girl's crayon sign, this door had a piece of paper taped to it, a name written in childish block letters. When I tried to read it, the letters scrambled and blurred as if I were in a dream.

From behind the door came a *clunk-clunk clunk-clunk* like cracking wood. I turned the knob and let myself in, finding a young boy in much the same position the little girl had been in, seated on the floor in a circle of toys, action figures and race cars, dominos and an assortment of wooden blocks. It was the same boy from the photos. The remembrance of his ugly contortion in the final picture made me wince. He was okay now. He banged two wooden blocks together, *clunk-clunk clunk-clunk*.

"Hey," I said, "what have you got there?"

His face was downturned. He stared at the blocks, *clunk-clunk clunk-clunk*.

I knelt. "What's your name, pal?"

He would not look at me, kept crashing his blocks, *clunk-clunk clunk-clunk*.

"Can you tell me what this place is?"

He smashed the blocks faster, *clunk-clunk clunk-clunk clunk-clunk*.

"Come on, kid, talk to me." I reached for him, thinking to take away one of his blocks and gain his attention. The kid was so despondent, sitting all alone in the night. Seeing him like that made me depressed. What was he doing in such a grim, forgotten place?

He screamed before I could touch him, opened his mouth and released a blood-curdling wail. He dropped his blocks and threw a temper tantrum, slapped his knees, screamed. Then he snapped his head up and looked at me, eyes fogged with tears. He looked so familiar. I wanted to hold him, to soothe him.

"It's alright," I said. "I'll get you out of this place." I touched his wrist, hoping it would stifle his drawn-out wail. Instead his skin burnt my hand and I reeled back. "Ow, what the fuck?"

The place where I had touched his skin glowed the bright orange of hot steel. The orange spread up his

Trial 23

arm, the sleeve of his shirt, his neck, until it covered his face and the boy radiated orange like an atomic child. He kept glowing brighter and brighter, moaning so loud I tipped over and covered my ears. He flared in a terrific climax of light, a huge burst of orange that blinded me.

It took a second to get my vision back. I rubbed my eyes grumbling. The boy's shriek had evaporated. I was astounded to find him petrified in stone, cold and dull with his mouth open in a soundless scream.

I sat bewildered, staring at the statue of the boy. It felt like I had somehow failed him. There he was, imprisoned in stone on the floor, and I could do nothing to help. My touch, I thought. Maybe the warmth of my hand would free him from his shell. But when I stroked his cheek the boy disintegrated. He crumbled into fine dust and his ashes slipped through my fingers.

I was left alone in the child's room with a pitiful feeling in my gut, sorrow and emptiness. I hated it in there. I hated the boy's bed, his bookshelf, his stupid fucking toys, his childhood stuffed between four walls. I couldn't stand it. I collected myself and went back into the hall.

Darkness pressed upon me from the right. It had swallowed the corridor. The only way forward was deeper down the hall, towards a pulsing light at its end. I had to shield my eyes against the brightness as I walked to it.

Then came the heat, a warm breeze wafting from the end of the passage. The air grew sultry and thick, the breath of a hot furnace. The closer I crept, the brighter the incandescence. It was a fire. It had to be. I could hardly see for the flare of it, sweating as I moved along.

I fell, tripped over an unseen edge and the

sensation was of passing through a great gust of heat. I landed on my back and was staring up at a wall of flame. It was a ring of fire. I was in a circular pit surrounded by flames. I stood and brushed myself off, then moved towards its core, where someone sat on an old dirty sofa watching a gameshow.

It was surreal, the same sofa from the photos in the middle of the circus ring, the flames heaving ten-feet tall. I heard the tv host, "We'll be back after these messages." And the tv cut out. The only sound was the whooshing of the fire. Then the man's voice, "What are you doing here, boy?" I could see the back of his head above the couch, a clump of shaggy black hair.

"Where is this place?" I asked.

"Damnation," he said. "Have you come to join me?"

I didn't like his tone. The man's voice was the grizzled buzz of a huge talking insect. "I want to leave," I told him.

"Where do you want to go, boy?"

I didn't know. I could think of no other place that existed other than where I was, at the bottom of nowhere. "Away from here."

He laughed, raucous and deep. "You will never leave this place." The man stood to face me, and that was when I recognized him. He was the same man from the kitchen, the same abomination who had beaten the woman within an inch of her life. He wore the same imitation face, his soggy mask. He had hairy beastlike arms and wolf's feet. "I am lord of the unhallowed depth," he said, "and you are forgotten."

He came towards me, lumbering with an animalistic gait. I had no place to run, no place to hide. I bolstered my legs and firmed my shoulders, ready for a fight with the shapeshifting freak. He was changing again. His façade melted to reveal the face of a withered old man, sunken eyes and a white wispy beard. He looked feeble. His wolf hair shed and beneath was an emaciated body riddled with bed sores, blotched and pathetic. It was difficult to feel afraid of the walking corpse.

But then he burst into flame, spontaneous human combustion. He marched onwards totally engulfed in fire. "You will burn in the halls of the forgotten," he said, and there was nothing feeble about his voice.

He was close to me now. His flame was dying, cooking his flesh. It slowly receded and what remained was the lord of the inferno in his purest form, body build of hot coal, a humanistic chassis of cinder. Two burning eye sockets without eyes, torso pocked and black, smoldering, bestrewn with pits of glowing coral and shallows of grey ash. He sprinted the short distance between us and shoved me to the ground with incredible force. I lay on my back, the molten beast standing above me. "I will burn away your soul, leave nothing to be remembered."

I was too frightened to do a damn thing, cowardly as he climbed onto me with rocky limbs that scorched every spot they touched. I cried out, "It burns!" As he grabbed hold of my face, cauterizing my flesh with his smoldering hands.

"You are forgotten," he said, and I saw down his crusted throat to the red-hot core at his center, the burning rock that was his heart. The embers he had for eyes flared and he raised his arm, fist of stone set to pulverize my face.

Something large moved behind him. My eyes were teary from the heat and it was hard to see. I caught a glimpse of gold, saw huge, steely talons grab the demon by his head and crush it like a clump of dirt. Fine grain and hot power sprinkled onto my face, got in my eyes and blinded me. I heard bursting rock, felt tiny stones raining onto me as the demon was destroyed.

And that was when I woke to the blinding light of my cell. I guess they do turn the lights off for a few hours at night. When they came on, I awoke from my crazy nightmare. I woke up and my whole body was hot.

The weirdest part was I had been fluid in the dream, emotional, having thoughts and feelings. It had not been a confusing pile of imagery and nonsensical delusions as a dream should be. This one had been substantial with purpose, almost designed. There had been a method to the madness, some deeper meaning that escaped me upon waking.

Stranger still was that while roaming from room to room in the depressing hallway, my only memory was of the previous nightmare when I had been manhandled by the beaten woman. Both dreams had boasted the same crusted demon, the bastard with the mush face. There must be a link between them. Yes, I can feel it, a connection between the two episodes. If I dream tonight, will a third chapter be revealed? Will I witness the next stage in the family's degeneration? I can't help but feeling like I know them, the violent dysfunctionals. Could they be…

Best not to think about it. My stomach is growling, I'm starved. It must be close to breakfast. I hope someone brings me something to eat soon.

Trial 23

Boris Chapman's personal log: October 25/10

We thought he'd be a fucking wreck by now. We watched Windhelm's new patient on the monitor last night. He paced his room, flailed his arms, climbed onto his bed and screamed into the air vent. But when we opened his door this morning to escort him to the cafeteria, the fucking cocksucker was fine! What gives? It's been three days. Why the fuck isn't he delusional? Damnit, I lost ten dollars to Edgar. I had my money on day three.

Windhelm told us the new guy would be his final subject. He told us he had perfected whatever the fuck he's trying to do. But we know Windhelm. The guy's a quack. He orders us to slip drugs into these fuckers' food and within days they've gone off the deep end. They rave like the rest of these retards. I think he's feeding them LSD. I asked Edgar if he wanted to try some, but the little bitch wouldn't. And I don't fucking dare. You won't catch me blithering in one of these cells.

The point is, Windhelm's new patient is fine. He walked with us to the cafeteria, all fucking content and smiley. What the fuck for? Fuck him. Fuck Windhelm too. I gave the kid extra in his lunch meal. What happened? He fucking froze! He zonked out for ten minutes, staring dead-eyed at the end of the cafeteria. Then he started blinking real fast. He looked around, kind of confused, brushed it off and

Harold Kish

finished his meal and we took him back to his cell. What a dick!

The last girl was way more fun, patient 7047. Edgar had liked her a lot. Windhelm's instructions were to keep a close eye on her. We sure did. Real close. The bitch had gotten into an accident at work, something about her brain and a forklift. She couldn't remember who she was. We kicked the shit out of Murphy next door and whispered things to her through the air vent, told her she was in Hell, she needed to get naked because her clothes were full of bugs. We tripled her dosage, whatever those white pills are that Windhelm gives us to feed to them. We watched on the monitors while she bugged out, totally fucking freaked. Then we went in and played with her. We had a real good time. I can still hear her screams.

She killed herself later, day four, stabbed a fucking pen straight through her eye. Dug scrubbed the tapes of Edgar and I fooling around. He always does. He's paid up. Dug earns a good wage keeping his filthy mouth shut about what Edgar and I do in this place. Windhelm thinks he's in charge. He has no fucking idea.

It's the old cunt's fault anyway. The guy's a quack, a stupid fucking eccentric. Windhelm stays all day in his lab, tinkering and fucking around. He has no idea we've botched all his experiments, tormented his patients and drugged them for fun. Fuck him. What does he expect? He hired us straight out the clink. I had just finished an eight-year term for murder. Edgar was out after two bids for aggravated sexual assault. We were in the rehabilitation program at the same time looking for security work. Along came Windhelm looking for

Trial 23

thugs. I guess he thought we'd be handy for his more unruly patients, those fuckers down in the dungeon.

    Whatever, the new guy will lose his marbles tomorrow. None of these fuckers last long at Wentworth.

Harold Kish

October 25th, Day 3

It happened again.

The eggheads came to fetch me for breakfast soon after my original entry of today. They snickered in the doorway as if they held some cruel secret between them. Rancid, beady-eyed pricks.

They delivered me to the cafeteria. I felt okay considering the circumstances. I caught myself smiling a few times while he walked, thinking about Mr. Clean and Mr. Strong lathered in oil, their hairless bodies entwined and silky as they kissed each other in a bathtub. It made me laugh to imagine it.

The cafeteria was insane with noise. I walked in to find my psychotic neighbors gathered in their feeding hall. Not quite 243, but close. Perhaps a hundred maniacs rocked at their tables with varying looks of horror, confusion, distress, simple lunacy. Some were sullen, looking bleakly at their trays of food. Others wept. Others ate with their hands and were clearly deranged.

It had me wondering what types of patients were brought to Wentworth Psychiatric Hospital. The people in the cafeteria were obviously beyond the realm of anything curable, anything sufferable. They were mad, all of them. Scratching themselves, bickering with ghosts, picking their noses. They were lost souls, the craziest people in existence. It occurred to me then that Wentworth's not an ordinary psychiatric hospital at all,

Trial 23

nor even a hospital, but a respite for deluded saps with no homes, no minds to function with. Wentworth's a goddamn flophouse for the clinically insane.

What the hell am I doing there?

Mr. Clean nudged me to the food counter where a skinny old hag glared at me, a lump of black hair sagging in her hairnet like a dead possum. She said nothing as she reached under the counter and brought out a tray of slop for me. There was a faded panther tattoo on her neck, some dude's name inked on her collar bone. Why is everyone in Wentworth so wretched? The woman looked like a trash bag alcoholic.

I took my food tray and Mr. Clean grinned at me. It was pure evil, like he knew something I didn't. "Enjoy," he said, and went to go stand guard by the door.

Where to sit amongst a hundred wild-eyed monkeys? I picked the table with the fewest crazies, took a seat and poked at my food. It was just mush, grey mush. Mush and hard bread and moldy green soup. I ate it. The guy across from me chewed his lips nervously and kept ogling me. It freaked me out. They all did. Everyone had their own special brand of madness. The old-timer by the window who winced at nothing and was visibly afraid of whatever demons he imagined were taunting him. The lady who spooned soup into her mouth and let it dribble off her chin. All of them were afflicted, minds terribly in ruin. It made me uncomfortable, even more concerned to be a prisoner amongst them. Surely there must be a better place for amnesiacs.

"Hey, you." The guy across from me leaned over the table, looking way too serious. He whispered, "He's coming. Look out, man, he's coming." Talking like the fucking Nazis were on their way to round us up. Hard to miss the frantic paranoia in his eyes.

I humored him. "Who's coming?"

"The Eater."

"Who's the Eater?"

He made a face like I was stupid. "The Eater, man. He comes for our souls."

I wanted to laugh. But he had this look about him, this dire mania. I kept my laugh to myself. I didn't want to get jabbed in the eyeball with a fork. "I'll be careful," I told him.

"Careful?" He was excited. "You can't be careful, man. He's the Eater. He comes for our souls." He chewed on his lip, hard enough to draw blood. "We've got to get out of here, man."

He was young, less than thirty. He was so desperate in his paranoia that I became immersed in it. "How?" I said. "How do we escape?"

"You don't remember?" He spoke in panicked shrieks. "You don't remember the way?"

"No. Do you?"

"I used to, man, but I forgot. I thought you'd remember. Why don't you remember?"

"Hey, calm down. I can't even remember who I am."

"Oh god." He scratched his face. "We're done for, man. The Eater's coming. He comes for our souls."

"Take a deep breath," I told him. "Try to relax." The guy's face was so red, so stressed, he looked ready to pop. "Take it easy." And before I could say more, the lights started to flicker.

Really flicker. They went nuts. It was a power surge. The lights spasmed and the lunatics screamed bloody murder. The guy across from me was convulsing, eyes rolled in the back of his head. I looked around for some sign of order, to see what the eggheads were doing, but they were gone.

Then the bulbs burst in a series of loud pops, the sprinkle of glass hitting the tables. When it was over,

Trial 23

only a few bulbs still worked, leaving the room cold and dim, somehow damp.

And it was silent. None of the patients made a sound. The madman across from me had gone stiff, looking at me bug-eyed. He mouthed, *The Eater, he comes.*

Cold fear crept into my bones. The guy had me spooked, had somehow compelled me into his delusion. I was suddenly nervous, paranoid in the clammy stillness of the cafeteria. What kind of villain had the power to stifle the ravings of a hundred frantic droolers? I didn't want to find out. The patients were unnaturally still, holding their breaths, waiting for a dramatic ball to drop. All I could hear was the sputter of electricity, the few flickering lightbulbs.

That was when I noticed something strange about the metal hatch at the back of the cafeteria. It didn't belong, was better suited in a dingy alley beside a dumpster. It's fold-out doors were violent, sinister. It had all the charm of a serial killer's hideout, a meat locker filled with bodies. I could not understand why it was jutting horizontally from the rear wall of the cafeteria.

It was the Eater who crawled from the hatch. I heard his footsteps thumping upwards on metal stairs. Everyone winced when the twin doors whooshed open and banged onto the floor. I thought I would piss myself when he appeared from the abyss. No wonder the patients were so frightened. The Eater was a freak. A terrifying freak.

And undeniably evil. Short and hobbled, dressed in black rags. Dripping, his grey skin perpetual moist, soggy to look at. He was frail and corpse-like. Two yellow slits gleamed within his droopy hood, menacing despite the Eater's short stature, his decaying limbs. He was riddled with IVs, syringes stuck into the tops of his veiny feet, his thin wrists, the interior creases of his elbows. Clear plastic tubes looped from his IVs to underneath his rags, filled with toxic neon liquid.

The Eater paced the room, all those tubes stuck into his gross body rustling. He pulled behind him a two-wheeled dolly with an oxygen bottle strapped to it, fixed to more tubes, supplying the Eater his vile green ink. It creaked as he dragged it behind him, moving through the aisles of frightened patients, sniffing one and moving to the next. I thought he was hunting.

From within his rags, the Eater retrieved a very thin blade. He used it to poke a man in the shoulder, sink it slowly into his muscle as if to check his tenderness. The man's face went tight. He bit his lip. Blood blossomed on his white hospital shirt and somehow, he stayed quiet, didn't squeal or scream or anything.

The Eater moved on to someone else, a middle-aged man, maybe forty-five, clean shaved with no obvious marks of his insanity. Yet he howled like a madman when the Eater prodded him in the shoulder with his knife. He couldn't help it. "Yooow, it hurts!"

The Eater's voice was a hiss. "Are you scared?" He leaned in close and sniffed the man. "Yes, I can smell it. You stink of fear. Juicy, tasty fear."

Of course he was scared! He quivered, had tears streaming down his face. The grey-rotted fuck had a knife stuck in his damn shoulder. Of course he was terrified! Everyone in the room was scared shitless.

"Good, give me your fear," the Eater said, and stabbed him again.

The man let loose a shrill yelp, his terror spiking. As he screamed, the Eater spread his palms over the man, cast some arcane spell, some necromancer's demon magic. The poor fucker howled like he had been set on fire and a greenish mist began to excrete from his flesh.

Trial 23

He wilted, thinned, was sucked dry, gradually condensing as his corporeal self was wrenched out of him in a green shroud. The Eater grinned and the man's essence was sucked into the Eater's tank in a stream of viridian spores. The man slumped dead in his chair, emaciated, looking like a shriveled-up mummy.

The guy across from me had peed. I could smell it. His eyes were squeezed shut and he mumbled prayers under his breath. It was much the same for the other patients. No one wanted to be noticed. Their heads were hung as they tried to remain invisible, as the Eater pulled his dolly about the room, sniffing people, basking in their fear.

He found a woman he liked, some young girl I hadn't noticed before. She had red hair and freckles. He snatched her by the hair and pulled her off her chair. She started screaming. "No, I'd rather die!"

The Eater laughed, a wheezy chuckle. He was a smaller, creepier version of the Grim Reaper. "Slowly," he said, "very slowly."

Then he dragged her across the room to his cellar, one dead hand in her hair and the other pulling his soul-tank. She screamed the whole way. "I'd rather die! Kill me! Please kill me!" No one intervened, not even me. I was crippled like the rest. The Eater stepped into his vault, the woman kicking wildly as she was pulled into the darkness. "Don't let him take me!"

Then she was gone into the Eater's abyss, whatever dank recess he called home, and her pleas were stifled as the hatch doors folded shut in a loud bang.

I couldn't comprehend what had happened. So fast and visceral, so intense. I looked to the wacko in front of me, clearly relieved to still be alive. "Not this time," he said. "The Eater came. He took their souls. He didn't take mine." His smile reminded me of something my useless brain could not capture. He was handsome, I thought. He had a lot of life.

Then the lights flickered, strobed intensely for about five seconds and everything returned to normal. The uproar of a hundred squalling mental patients deafened me and the brightness of the lights blinded me. I blinked, gave my head a shake. The guy in front of me was much older now, grey bush of a beard, some unknown psychosis playing behind his eyes. He was a different person! He ogled me and it freaked me out. The rest of the patients freaked me out, their tantrums, their hair pulling. What happened to the Eater? Where was the man's wilted husk?

It took asking myself these questions to figure out the answer. It jolted me. A dream, I realized. I had slipped into another dream. My expression turned dumb and I must have looked as lost as the kooky old man across from me. I could not remember falling asleep. Do I have fucking narcolepsy? My reality had crumbled, gave way to a volatile yet believable dreamscape without a hiccup. I never even suspected I was dreaming. It had come and gone seamlessly, real life coalesced with some dark part of my buried subconscious and then faded away. How long had I been out? A minute? Two?

Now I had questions. The first time in Dr. Mandalay's machine could have been exhaustion, lulled to sleep by the mechanical whirr. The second dream could have been a dream; it had been at night. But this? A snap episode over breakfast? I felt hot, anxious, scared for my sanity. I finished the rest of my grey mush with bugs creeping up my spine. Am I more insane than the doctors have led me to believe? Is this some elaborate rouse? I thought they had brought me to Wentworth to help recover my memories. It's been three days since I woke up. No one has helped me remember jackshit.

Trial 23

I'm carted around this depressing grave of a hospital as a prisoner. Why is no one helping me?

On my way out of the cafeteria, still jittery from my dark reverie, I kept glancing at the back of the room where the Eater's hatch had been. Nothing there anymore. I shuffled out amongst a throng of babbling blowfish fucks, sputtering idiots, and there was no hatch, just a wall.

Mr. Clean took me to my cell, more disgruntled than usual. His sneers were mean. His annoyance weighed heavy in the hallways as we walked. At my cell, he nudged me inside rather aggressively. "Fuck you," he said, and slammed the door, locking me once again in my eternal chamber of light.

It must be four in the afternoon now. I've been sitting here for hours. My head hurts. No one came to feed me at lunch. All I can think about are these damn dreams, maybe because there is nothing else housed in my brain. The dreams feel as real as this hospital, yet are more interesting, more vivid. I find myself wondering what happened to the family. Was that it? They combusted in one night of violent abuse and were gone? And who's the Eater? Where did he come from? What does he have down in his cellar?

I must be crazy for pondering these things, but I have nothing except time and my imagination. Where's the goddamn doctor to help free my memories? Where are you, Windhelm?

Harold Kish

The Journal of Dr. W. Windhelm. Dated 25th of October, the year 2010.

A tragic childhood reveals itself through the dark shroud in John's mind. A hellish childhood, as John described it. He manifested his own father as a cinder demon, built of ash and fire. He must have hated his father so fiercely that not even John's fantasy could recreate his face. His hatred masked his father, had him veiled in a pudgy inhuman façade.

Hard to decipher the fate of John's mother, his sister. Ravens and abuse. Whatever happened to John as a child was so terrible, so traumatizing, even with the help of my procedure the truth disguises itself. He still does not remember. His broken mind will not allow it.

Yet time will yield results. John is impotent now, dredged in worry, in fear of his own sanity; and by every right. A new nemesis has replaced the molted face of his father. The Eater, John calls him, the hooded cretin of grey flesh feasting on the fears of others. I

Trial 23

have several hypotheses for the yellow-eyed monster's identity but would rather not speculate. I will wait until tomorrow, until after I reassure John that I am doing all I can to help recover his memory. Perhaps a walk through the courtyard will ease his mind, some fresh air. At dinner time, I will sneak into John's cell once more while he eats and read his journal.

It is truly a spectacle, the power of the mind, the power of my creation to create, to coerce John's inner demons into his reality. His trial is already going better than the others. His progress is made in blips and flashes, small segments of muddled memory mutated into something hideous, something scary for John to overcome. Imagine it, to give a man the ability to construct his own fantasies, overlap them with the real world, to walk amongst the dead and shape the universe at will. And the flip side, to shun a person into insanity without them ever knowing it.

The truth of the power I have created will become clear in the next few days as John strays deeper down the rabbit hole and his journey intensifies. I can hardly wait to see the results. It is like a book, the story of John's life told in a psychedelic freakshow.

Lastly, I must speak with Boris. How dare he curse at my patient. How dare he not bring John his lunch this afternoon. I knew it was a mistake to hire convicts. I should replace Boris and Edgar with more professional staff from St. Clemency. They have always made me uneasy. Then again, perhaps I can find a suitable trial for the "eggheads", as John so happily describes them. Even degenerates like Boris and Edgar may serve a purpose.

October 26th.

Doctor Windhelm summoned me to his office after breakfast, a breakfast which had been significantly less terrifying than yesterday's. No dreams or hallucinations. No monsters from hell. Only me and a hundred shit-flingers. Mush and dry bread and noisy lunatics. It was a relief when Mr. Clean snatched me from my table. "Boss wants to see you." And him and Mr. Strong led me down the hall to Windhelm's office.

It was the same as the first time, musty, infiltrated by rich tobacco. Windhelm sat behind his desk chewing on a stogie, looking like Black Beard in his captain's quarters. Wood paneling, desk cluttered with maps and documents and odd trinkets. He said, "Hello, John. Take a seat."

I did, feeling much calmer this time. I was hungry for answers and intended to get them.

"How are you?" he asked.

But I figured he already knew exactly how I was feeling. The stress showed in my face, it must have. The irritation in my eyes from lack of sleep, the strain from the goddamn lights in my cell. I had woken annoyed, and I answered Windhelm with annoyance.

"Bad," I said. "I am bad. I thought you were going to help with my amnesia. Instead you've abandoned me, locked me in my cell twenty hours a day. I've been bullied by your bald goons, subjected to driveling lunatics, and fed nothing but pig shit. I am bad, Doc. Real bad. I want answers."

He grumbled, studying me through his huge spectacles. "You are stressed, dear boy." He opened a desk drawer. "Your eyes are bloodshot." And retrieved a small tin container, opened it and placed two white pills in front of me. "Take these. They will get rid of your headache and help you relax."

"I'm still mad," I said, taking the pills. "I don't belong here." I popped them in my mouth, snapped my head back and dry-swallowed. "This place is for lunatics, real fuckjobs. All I have is amnesia, doctor. I should be in a normal hospital. I think I should talk to someone, maybe a lawyer. Don't I have a phone call?"

Windhelm just stared at me, puffed on his cigar. His unflinching gaze made me feel like a child, like I was small and stupid. He completely dodged everything I had said. "Tell me, John, do you remember anything yet?"

"No, but—"

"I would like to help. Perhaps a brief session together. Allow me to utilize some of the older tactics, do a bit of deep mind probing. We may yet unearth something."

"Okay, but I still think—"

"Dear boy, could you take a seat on the couch for me?"

Windhelm rose abruptly on a plume of cigar smoke. He was a broad man, thick chested and husky. I did as he asked, slinked from my chair onto the couch beside the bookcase. "I really want to talk about a lawyer," I said, stretching out on the couch. It was very comfy.

Windhelm brought a chair over, sat above me and crossed his legs. He had a small notepad. "Tell me, John, what do you remember about your childhood?"

I couldn't believe it. He was disregarding everything I said! "Nothing. I told you, I can't remember."

"What about your father, John. Can you remember his face? Think hard. Concentrate."

"No, nothing. What about the lawyer?"

Windhelm lifted his glasses, rubbed his face and sighed. "John, a lawyer can do nothing for you. I want you to listen to me. Take a deep breath and close your eyes. Picture your family in your head. Try to imagine them. Close your eyes and concentrate."

What a sham. How was I supposed to concentrate when Windhelm was clearly manipulating me, using evasion tactics and blowing his stinky cigar smoke over my face? I closed my eyes and frowned. "This is bullshit. I can't remember anything. Why won't you acknowledge my concerns?"

"Hush, John. Sink into the void in your mind. Let the pictures form."

"Fine." I exhaled deeply. It was comfortable in the doctor's chair and I quickly relaxed. Perhaps it was the pills. I began to sink, to drift through the space in my mind. I entered a void, but in it were no images, not of anyone. My head was empty. Then my eyelids dimmed as if Windhelm had turned off the lights.

"Doctor?"

Nothing. I opened my eyes to a darkened office. Windhelm was gone. Standing in the shadows was the man from the cafeteria, the young guy who had warned me about the Eater. Only now he wore jeans and a denim jacket, his short hair styled, looking ready for a night out. But his attitude was all wrong. He sulked in the dimness of Windhelm's office and dragged on a smoke.

"What are you doing here?" I asked him.

He paced, smoked, talked to himself. "Where the hell are you? Fuck's taking you so long?"

"Hey, are you alright?"

He couldn't hear me. He didn't know I was there. "Every fucking time." Still pacing, head down, smoking nervously. "Never again, man. Never fucking again."

He was making me anxious, moving back and forth across Windhelm's dusky office, looking right, looking left. "Come on, man. Where are you? It's fucking late." And then he stopped. He looked straight at me—no, through me. His face twisted in revulsion. "What the fuck do you want? Hey, get away from me. Stop that. Hey motherfucker, back up. Hey!"

A shot went off, a blast of light and a scream. The lights in Windhelm's office flashed on and the guy evaporated with the shadows.

Windhelm was muttering in his chair, "Yes, that is quite well for today."

I sat upright. "What just happened?" In a cold sweat, confused.

"You did well, John." Windhelm got up and moved across the room, left me sweating. "You really dug into your subconscious, lubricated the hinges of the locked compartment where your memories are stored." He slumped into his office chair, began to fiddle with papers. "Yes, next time we will delve deeper, try to open that door. But you did well. Very well."

I stood up. "What are you talking about?"

He wouldn't even look at me. Windhelm shuffled through papers. "Take a walk in the courtyard, dear boy. Let your mind relax. That was a hard session for you."

I gaped, stuttered. "But...what..." Windhelm was acting like we had just finished an hour-long therapy session, like he had fucking hypnotized me. Had I fallen asleep in his chair? Impossible! My eyes had been closed for less than a minute before everything

Trial 23

changed. What the hell was going on?

But before I could get the words out, Windhelm had called for the orderlies. Mr. Strong and Mr. Clean barged into the room, seized me by my elbows. "Take John to the courtyard. Give him an hour to stretch his legs." He finally looked up at me. "We have made progress, John. You did well today."

And that was it. I dug my heels into the carpet and the eggheads had to manhandle out of the good doctor's office.

It should have been nice. The courtyard was green, full of flowers, bordered by nice trees. The sun was out. Crazy seniors meandered hopelessly down the cobbled walkways. But I was mad. Windhelm had blown me off, straight-up snubbed me. And his fucking pills were not working. I wasn't calm. I was agitated and unruly. He was supposed to be a doctor, a goddamn professional. Instead Windhelm had acted like a conman, condescending and downright manipulative. I wanted to know what had happened on his couch. I thought I was losing my mind.

That was when he sidled up beside me, as I made my way through the flower garden. It was pretty in the courtyard, bees and butterflies hovering over the flowers. "Hey, man. Tough day?"

I looked. There he was, walking beside me, the same guy from Windhelm's office, from the cafeteria. He was young and cool, gelled hair, denim jacket. "Yeah," I said to him. "A long day. Four long days, actually."

"Every day is long when you can't remember. I've been stuck here for ages, man, waiting for you."

"I'm sorry," I said, "but I don't know who you are."

"You do." He sounded sure of it, and his certainty annoyed me. We walked along and the guy had his hands stuffed in his pockets, sullen, the way his head was hung. "You've just forgotten, man. You need to remember."

I was sick of people telling me to remember. Windhelm still had me on edge, had me in an explosive mood. "It's not that fucking easy," I told the guy. "I don't know my name, who I am, where I've been. I know nothing about my life. What even is this place?"

We had walked through the garden and into a street, a nighttime avenue walled by shuttered businesses and degraded apartment buildings. It was a rough part of town, I could tell. Everything was dingy, even the streetlamps. There was a bar down the block from us, a few solemn assholes loitering outside.

"Graton Ave, dude." The guy lit a smoke, walked into the middle of the road and held up his arms. "The shittiest street in town. My favorite. Yours too, last time I checked."

I didn't recognize the place. It was hollow and dead, more of a gutter than a street. "I hate it here," I told him. "I want to leave."

"Jack's is just down there." He pointed at the bar, its red neon sign. "Just a block away, man. You don't remember?"

I was getting uncomfortable, nervous, my skin starting to prickle. I really hated the look of the bar, the seediness of the street. I wanted to go back to the garden, but when I looked behind me there was nothing, a void of blackness. "Take me back," I said. "Take me back to the hospital."

"What hospital, man? Let's go to Jack's. Come on." And he came to me, gave me a friendly pat on the back. "You look shook, man. You need a drink."

"I want the hospital."

He frowned. "Hospital, are you nuts?" Looking at me like I was an alien with three eyes. "No, man.

Trial 23

What you want is a drink. Come on."

He tried to pull me with him down the street. "Let's go." But I didn't like it. I hated his touch, his aggression, the way he talked to me like he knew me. I was already wound up and mad, and I panicked. I pulled away from him, spun and clocked the guy in the jaw. The smack of my knuckles against his flesh was liberating.

"The fuck?" He stumbled back holding his face. He was horrified, in perfect awe. "Are you fucking crazy, man?"

"I'm not crazy!" I charged, sick of it all, sick of the frightening places, my own confusion, this stubborn bastard continuously popping up uninvited. I hit him in the nose and he fell flat on his ass. "Leave me alone!"

"You've gone nuts, man. Don't you know who I am? Don't you know what you're doing?" Blood flowed down his nose. "You're fucking on one, man. Your bonkers."

I took a step and gave him a swift kick under his chin, snapped his head back and it cracked against the pavement. "I'm not crazy!" I brought my foot down on his temple. "I'm not!" And stomped on his face until it softened. I stamped his head into the pavement until his skull dented, concaved, then broke apart like a crushed melon. "I'm not insane!" Smearing his collapsed face, his scraps of hair and skull, the flattened jelly of his brain. "I'm sane, damnit! I'm sane!"

Boris Chapman's personal log: October 26/10

That was hard to watch, even for a murdering fuck like me. I knew Windhelm's patient would lose it. Day four, baby. I fucking knew it. What I didn't expect was how explosive it would be. Brutal, a fucking jailhouse slaughter.

    He was in a bad mood when we dragged his limp ass out of Windhelm's office, heels dug into the carpet like a fucking child. I don't know what the doctor did to him, what he said to make him so angry, but he came out of the boss's office in a tizzy. He didn't look nuts to me, not on our way to the courtyard. He looked mad, like a guy does on his first day in the joint, pissed at the whole world for locking him up, bug-eyed as fuck. That shit I can sympathize with.

    But then we let him loose in the courtyard. Windhelm's patient marched around with his head down, mumbling to himself, kicking at the grass. He looked crazy then, like a wacko with a mean temper. He bumped into Bernie. Bernie's an old coot. Er, was an old coot, had a nasty snap of dementia. Mostly talked to himself. Him and Windhelm's boy walked side by side through the garden, both twats yacking to themselves. It was the strangest fucking thing. Both dudes were lost in their own fucked up minds. I poked Edgar. "Hey, this is it, Windhelm's pushed his boy over the edge."

Trial 23

Neither of us expected him to sucker-punch Bernie in the fucking jaw. Then a jab to Bernie's nose. The old coot shrieked, blood flew, and Windhelm's patient was on him. "I'm not crazy!" He screamed. Yeah right. He mashed Bernie's head. Really fucking mashed the old bugger. Stomped his head in good. Edgar and I watched until Bernie's face was slush on the cobble walkway, his skull fucking flattened.

"I'm sane, damnit! I'm sane!" He yelled at Bernie's creamy brains.

Edgar and I had to get him the hell out of there before he caused a riot. The other patients freaked. Patty, the lunch hag, came out screaming. It was fucking anarchy in the courtyard. We wrangled the howling fuck while he kicked and screamed, "I'm not crazy! I'm not!" But he sure looked crazy. I saw straight into his eyes. The lights were on, but fuck, there wasn't nobody home.

We got him into the building and he kind of went limp. Edgar and I had to drag him to the place where bad boys go. He was dazed. All his fury was gone. He blinked, totally out of it. "It wasn't real," he said when we slumped him into the elevator. And I told him, "You're a cold-blooded killer, kid."

Now I knew he was crazy. He was fucking lost. "No, it was a dream. It's not real. It was a goddamn dream."

Edgar said, "Tell that to Bernie."

And Windhelm's boy folded over himself in the corner of the elevator and shivered. "What the fuck is happening to me?" It wasn't a question. Not really. He didn't intend for anyone to answer.

Then he asked, "Where are we going?"

"Level 2," I told him. "Down to the dungeons. You killed someone. You're fucked now, kid.

Welcome to Wentworth's asshole."

Trial 23

October 26th.

I'm not writing today's log from my cell. I'm writing from my dungeon. The eggheads dumped me here after my outburst in the courtyard and a couple hours later, someone slid a tray of food through a trap at the bottom of my door, a rickety metal thing from the Middle Ages. With my food was my journal and some pens. Apparently, Windhelm wants me to keep writing.

     This place must be part of the original structure of Wentworth, probably damn near a century old. It's a primitive dungeon, cold and clammy. There are bars on my window, the window itself high up and out of reach. All I can see is blackness. There is a metal bucket for pissing, for shitting. The whole cell reeks like feces. Old feces. There are scribblings on the wall. Something like,

    AlWays IN DarKnEsssS   (=)   Tomb-Tomb
        Where the sun?   THE DOCTOR IS MAD
~^~   XX11   72days-1 more
        LocK Him iN TherE Is NO EscАPe

     The scribblings of demented prisoners shunned here before me. How many? I can only guess. Hundreds, even thousands of tortured souls?

     I'm one of them now. No doubt they have locked me up and thrown away the key. I killed a man for god's sake. Physically crushed a man's head like a soggy pumpkin. His name was Bernie. That was what Mr. Strong said moments after Mr. Clean had called me a cold-blooded killer. It churns my guts to think about it, to remember the liquid sensation of my foot smooshing the man's head.

So, not a dream after all. It was more of a hallucination, more enhanced than a hallucination. My episode in the courtyard was a blend of fantasy and reality, a twisted matrix. Visions engrained over the template of what was real, so I walked and interacted with very tangible things (poor fucking Bernie) yet what I saw was drastically different.

Conclusion? I'm a fucking loon. I'm gonzo. I'm apeshit. It makes me wonder if I was ever an amnesiac. I have a strong feeling Doctor Windhelm avoided my concerns for one very upsetting reason: I am crazy, and everything he's saying to me is an elaborate rouse to… what, trick me into being sane?

I simply don't know. All hope is lost. Even after I murdered someone and was banished to this dungeon, I continued to cavort with the dream world. It just won't fucking end.

Egg-fuck one and egg-fuck two deposited me in this nightmare chamber, left me to coddle myself on the stone floor and sob for my missing sanity. Maybe an hour went by. I wrestled with what I had done, with the horrifying truth of how I had murdered an innocent man, an unfortunate soul whose only crime was to be insane and near me at the wrong time, caught in the crossfire of my rampant imagination. Dreams? Fuck that. More like walking nightmares, the delusions of a broken mind.

The door creaked open. I looked up from the ball I was curled in to see Windhelm standing in the doorway in a gaseous shroud of cigar smoke.

"You bastard," I said, scrambling to my feet. "What did you do to me?"

His face was vague, body no more than an

obscure shape in the swirling smoke, a fog portal to another dimension. I thought his cigar fumes were fueling the smog. He grinned and stepped backwards, a demonic red flash from behind his glasses, and Windhelm dissolved into the mist.

"Not so fast," I called after him. "You son of a bitch. What aren't you telling me?" And I chased the doctor through the foggy gateway.

It felt like pushing through a wall of foam. I struggled out of the cloud and found myself on a dark and vastly desolate street in the bitter chill of a winter's night. Windhelm was gone. There was no one. The faint scent of tobacco lingered in the cold air.

"Bastard," I said. Then I turned, thinking to move back through the fog portal and into my cell; but it was gone, sealed up by the brick façade of some shitty tenement. "Fuck." I was trapped in the moonless ghetto.

I stepped into the road. Down the block was the flickering neon sign for Jack's bar, the dumpy joint the guy whose brains I had creamed all over the road had tried coaxing me into for a drink. The sign fizzled red, bright on the otherwise bland and grimy avenue. I could hear the dead man's voice on the wind, *"Where are you? Hurry up?"*

No, not on the wind. He was in front of Jack's bar, pacing inside the yellow spotlight of a streetlamp, looking like the goddamn Marlboro Man. I could see him drawing on his cigarette, could hear him complaining. "Always fucking late. You're always fucking late, man. Hurry up."

"You're alive," I shouted down the street. But he didn't hear me, just kept pacing, kept smoking his cigarette.

"I'm coming." And I started down the road.

Yet as I moved, the way forward stretched and became impossibly distant. I was walking but the street kept getting longer. I shifted into a run. "I'm coming, man. Wait for me. I'm sorry I hit you." Excited to see him alive. I wasn't a murder after all. But the damn street kept elongating. I rushed beneath twisted lines of electric cables, past dripping awnings and wet gutters, charred brick buildings with rusty fire escapes. There was no end to it. I just kept sprinting through the ramshackle constructs of an inner city.

And his calls were getting frantic. "Come on, dude. Fuck. Hurry. It's cold out here. Where are you?"

Panic grew inside me. I yelled to him, "I'm close. I'm coming. Wait for me." But I got no closer. The street warbled and I could not reach him. I could see him perfectly in his little halo of light, and I saw the stunted stranger move into the light with him, a midget of a thing in a grubby coat.

He said, "Hey, get back. What are you doing? Fuck off, man. Get the fuck away from me. No. Wait. Don't!"

The flash of a gunshot and he crumpled onto the street. The grubby thing in its dark rags knelt and foraged through the guy's pockets, then sauntered into Jack's place.

And suddenly I was upon him. The street contracted and in five brisk steps I was kneeling at his body. "What happened?" But he was dead, a bullet through his gut, blood flowing into the sewer.

"You silly bastard." I looked at his pale face, recognizing him but unable to place it. He was deeply familiar. His handsome features, cold now in death. Lips that I knew could smile brightly, curled in a last expression of pain. I felt an immense amount of guilt. Seeing him dead made my soul hurt. Had I let this happen? I had tried to reach him, but the damn street hindered me. I didn't make it in time and now he was dead. Finitely dead, lifeforce weeping into the gutter.

Trial 23

I turned my attention on Jack's, the front door left ajar. I picked myself up. "Sorry, man." To the sad corpse. And chased the murderer into Jack's place.

There was no bar, only a dark stairwell. I leaned over the railing and saw the bottom a great way down, deep as a mineshaft. There was a gentle wash of light at the bottom of the steps.

I raced down them, feet hammering each metal stair. Halfway to the bottom I paused to look up, a void of swirling darkness like some horrible cave ceiling above me. I kept on, holding the rickety handrailing until I reached the floor.

An archway led out of the gloomy stairwell. I went beneath it and into a room that was somewhere between a torture chamber and a science lab, an ugly version of Doctor Frankenstein's laboratory. Ungodly machinery and the leftovers of human experiments.

There was an hourglass shaped tank at the back of the room. Its two sections were connected by a steel pipe. Each compartment of the hourglass had a foggy window, top chamber ¾ full of some icky green ichor, the bottom empty.

In front of the bizarre contraption was the Eater, hideously naked without his black rags. He was shriveled in a disgusting way, like a malformed fetus. His grey skin was slimy looking. Yellow slits in his taut face for eyes. Everywhere were needles. Stabbed into his hands, his feet, legs and arms, around his hips, one injected into the base of his bloodless worm. The tubes coming off them converged at his spine, at a storage pod grafted along his spinal column. He looked like a failed lab experiment, a bloated abortion kept alive by the device on his back. The tank he wore was 1/6 full of green slime. Perhaps that was what caused his atrophy. The Eater was low on juice.

He said nothing to me and went about his

business as if I wasn't there. He took a pair of long chains off a table and affixed them to either side of the hourglass on big steel rings. At the ends of the links were hooks. He took one in each hand and crossed his workshop, the chain links unwinding behind him, to an operating table in the middle of the room. Still, he ignored me.

Perhaps it was a fear tactic to leave me stunned in the threshold of his torture chamber. If the repository of green goo and the Eater's repugnant body was not enough to frighten me, the discarded corpses were. The place was a storehouse for the dead. Everywhere I looked were the mutilated remains of the Eater's victims. He had their raw materials stacked in heaps and mounds, fly-ridden cadavers and severed limbs, decapitated heads in the metal gutters that ran through the room, half an inch of stagnant blood in the wide trenches, drains clogged with bits of human. It chilled me to behold such carnage.

Then I saw the pens, the giant bird cages dangling from the dark cavity of the ceiling. Many held the dead and rotting. Some held skeletons. One held the red-haired woman I had witnessed stolen from the cafeteria by the Eater. She peeped at me through the bars of her cage, pale and ghostly, obviously afraid. She mouthed... *Run. Go away. Forget this place.*

I mouthed back, *Where?*

"Anywhere but here!" She rattled her cage, made it swing from its chain. "Forget you were ever here. Run, fool. Run from this place!"

The only thing that ran was my blood, fucking cold as the Eater looked up from his work and hissed, "Silence, creature. Your fear grows stale." He waddled to below her cage, looking so much like a giant mutated baby with an undeveloped face. "I've swallowed my fill of you," he said, and pulled a rusty lever on the floor.

Trial 23

A mechanism clunked and the floor of the woman's cage opened. She let out a shrill scream and fell, was jerked to a stop by a cord around her neck. She hung, swayed, choking to death. It scared me to watch her die. What scared me more was the mangled state of her body. Had the Eater done those things to her? One of the woman's arms was missing, left an infected stump. Her legs were sutured together using chicken wire, deformed to make her look like an abominable mermaid. Face beaten. Body lacerated, burned. There was a barbed wire corset wrapped around her breasts, drawing blood as she convulsed and died and went limp, swaying gently from the cord.

"What have you done?" I said to the Eater. I was afraid, but just as equally appalled. If I had any courage at all I'd have rushed the little goblin and clobbered his ugly face.

"Hush," he said, "and witness fear. Come closer."

My nerves sparked. I didn't want to take another step into the Eater's horror chamber. Yet I did. I crept forward, the Eater standing at the operating table, hooks resting on its surface and what was clearly a body laying underneath a white sheet.

"Are you afraid?" he asked, that same raspy whisper.

I gulped and said nothing. But it didn't matter. He knew I was afraid. He said, "Yes, I can smell it. You will drown in your fear, creature. Meat, flesh, food. You will be forgotten." In one dramatic motion, the Eater flung aside the sheet, revealing the cold and naked body of the man outside, the man who had been shot, the man whom I had stomped to slush. Although he lay dead on the table, he was far from at peace. His face was contorted in anger.

"Friend of yours?" the Eater asked. He smiled with his rotten gums.

"No," I said, though it felt like a lie. "I don't know this man."

"Nor will you." The Eater picked up his hooks. "Witness the power of fear." And plunged them into the corpse's eyeballs. "Behold!"

I did. I beheld it all. I saw the man's body shake as though electrified, his spirit summoned forth in a powerful green aura. His soul detached and hovered above his naked body. It screamed, "I can't see! I can't see! Where am I?" And the Eater was right. I did witness fear, true and incorruptible fear. The wraith attempted to fly away, to return to whatever ethereal plane he had been drawn from. Yet the hooks buried in his face kept him grounded. The ghost cried out in terror, chained to the hourglass.

The Eater was at his controls. He pulled a lever and the chains retracted, pulling the phantasm towards the hourglass chambers. The green spirit fought. He struggled against the chains like a genie fighting not to be summoned back into his lamp. Then he was ripped asunder. He yowled and his spectral form burst into a cloud of green vapor. The energy was absorbed into the chains, flowed up the links and turned the metal a vivid green. The essence was then sucked into the top chamber of the hourglass and deposited as liters and liters of thick green slime.

What had I just witnessed? A double murder? The death of a man and the execution of his spirit? I wanted to run, but the Eater wasn't finished. "Now," he said, "prepare to be banished from memory."

He disconnected the main tube from the tank on his spine and plugged it into a socket on the lower chamber of the hourglass, connecting his personal storage tank to the machine. Then he slapped a button on the control panel and the contraption grumbled to life. The upper chamber churned like a washing machine. The gunk mixed, bubbled, thickened; and it drained through the metal pipe into the bottom chamber. The Eater was giddy, clapping his hands as the fresh batch of ooze pumped through the main tube and into his storage tank, then was dispersed through the network of hoses that sprouted from his spinal column and into his veins.

I should have gotten out of there, at least backed out of the room. But the Eater was transforming. I couldn't look away. He gave a grunt, tensed and sputtered. His muscles were growing, getting huge and his veins bulged beneath his skin like bloated green leeches. I heard the cracking of bones as they rearranged, the Eater getting bigger, reforming himself into a humongous abomination, a seething beast with wide yellow eyes and a mouthful of railroad spikes.

It took maybe ten seconds for the Eater to morph into a giant. His head towered above me in the canopy of cages, his eyes glowing evilly in the darkness. He roared and thrashed, mad as a monster, and pulled one of the cages from the ceiling and threw it at me.

The cage barely missed, hit the ground near me and crashed into the wall. Then the Eater smacked a mound of bodies and sent them flying at me. Three missed, but one limp corpse skidded off the ground and swept my legs out from under me. My face hit the floor and I chipped my teeth, mouth gone numb. I lifted myself up and saw the Eater reach for the red-haired woman still hanging from her cable. He snatched her off it, the woman tiny in his hand like a doll. I scrambled to my feet just as he hefted her at me.

I ducked and her body sailed over my head and went straight through the archway and burst open like a bloody water balloon against the wall, left a red splatter over the concrete and the stairs.

I turned and ran.

The Eater made a great clamor as he chased after me, his pounding steps, the clatter of cages falling from the ceiling, the rustle of him knocking over the stacks of bodies. He was so huge! I passed beneath the archway, leapt over the redhead's mangled scraps and made for the stairs. But the bastard caught me. He had burst through the archway in hail of stone and snatched me by my leg. Bits of concrete crumbled from the ceiling and he dragged me to him, his head below the broken arch, saliva dripping off his spiked teeth. He was going to eat me!

"Please god no." I pushed off the floor with my one free foot, tried to flipper backwards with my elbows. It didn't matter. He was too strong, slowly pulling me into his mouth. "Please don't eat me!"

Just as I felt the moisture of his breath, as I was about to be stuffed into the behemoth's jaws, something huge crashed through the wall and tackled him. I saw a flash of black and gold, the sheen of metal, then the Eater was gone. My mysterious savior had tackled him deeper into his sick lab. I heard a crash, heard them fighting. I scrambled to my feet and made a break for it.

Heaving, I raced up the stairs. Even at the top I could hear their struggle, feel the structure crumbling apart as the two titans fought. I rammed the door with my shoulder and was gone.

I went from the top of the stairs straight into my dungeon cell. I was bewildered, out of breath, shaken to my core. I collapsed and started to cry.

It had been the realest yet, transitioning from falsity to reality without pause, without a stammer, without any indication. And I was left terrified, scared to go near the door, to look at the window, to close my eyes, to even think.

A few hours have passed since then and I feel a

Trial 23

little better. I ate. I got my notebook delivered to me. I've already rambled about my shattered psyche, about my despair at having killed a man, about my suspicions regarding Windhelm. I won't reiterate. I won't complain anymore. I will say only that I am lost, forsaken to decay in this underground hell. I killed a man. There is no saving me. There are only my delusions, the bizarre story being told through cryptic and nightmarish visions. And my savior, the beast with golden talons who has saved me twice. I wonder when I will see him again. Could he be the key to repairing my mind?

    I see moonlight outside my window and it calms me. It's somewhat refreshing to know I will never leave this place. I have nothing left to worry about, to look forward to. There's a voice inside me that says I deserve it. I don't know. Maybe I do. I'm at my lowest deep. It can't get any worse from here.

Margaret's Journal: 10/26/10

This experiment is out of control. Someone's dead. Bernie's dead. He was a sweet old man and our patient killed him. Because of what Windhelm and I have done, I had to go into the courtyard this afternoon and watch the cleaners scrub Bernie off the cobble walkway. Now John's in solitary confinement. The stooges have him locked in the basement. It's dreadful down there. It's cold and lonely, no plumbing or heating. There are only four others in the lower cells. They're the worst patients at Wentworth, violent people.

    John's not violent. I saw his gentle soul when I looked in his eyes. It's the procedure that has him disgruntled and lashing out. Windhelm told me what happened, that John slipped into an episode while on the doctor's couch. John was talking to someone who wasn't there. Windhelm, that bastard, didn't even give John an explanation. Then it happened again fifteen minutes later in the courtyard. John must have thought Bernie was someone else, someone from his developing world. He never knew Bernie was a harmless old man with dementia, a daughter who visits once a weekend and three lovely grandchildren. The guilt must be eating John alive.

    I really should tell him what's happening. The procedure is working, according to Windhelm. John's mind is gradually creating a world to overlap this one. That means our science is correct. We have engineered

Trial 23

a way to infuse fantasy with reality, to amplify one's thoughts into the real world. The prospects are amazing to consider. A controlled hallucination, a way to bring thoughts to life, to interact with the past, to graft entire realms over what the eyes can see. Just imagine it, practicing for a presentation before a false crowd, architects building entire houses with their minds on empty plots of land, filmmakers crafting a three-hour film in seconds with their imagination. It's incredible, just incredible. The ability to control dreams!

    But John doesn't know what's happening to him. He has no control. To him, it's just nightmares. John does not realize his past is being woven in cryptic visions. What if he becomes lost in them? What if he truly does go crazy? At least if I tell him, perhaps John can find some control. At least he won't think he's losing his mind. At least he won't jab a pen into his brain like 7047. But Windhelm refuses. He claims John must remain ignorant. Why? I don't understand. John is in ruins, trapped in the basement thinking he's a murderer, that he's experiencing terrible hallucinations. How does this help him?

    It doesn't. It's just another one of Windhelm's sick games. I'm tired of them. I'm tired of Windhelm. He's got his formula. I won't let him destroy John's mind. Tomorrow morning I plan to barge into Windhelm's office and demand that John be released.

Harold Kish

The Journal of Dr. W. Windhelm. Dated 27th of October, the year 2010.

Mandalay found her courage, what little of it she has. The little mouse barged into my office this morning after my meeting with Boris and Edgar. How dare she, spitting demands, barking orders. Does she know whose hospital this is? Mine. Wentworth is mine.

"John needs our help," she said, standing timid in the middle of my office. Margaret always was a skittish creature from the first day I hired her. "You can't keep him locked in the basement, doctor. You can't. He's in a very fragile state of mind. We should tell him about the procedure before he loses himself. He thinks he killed a man."

"He did kill a man," I said. "He bludgeoned Bernie's skull with his foot. I watched the tape yesterday, witnessed John's murderous fury firsthand. It was impressive. Boris and Edgar were only doing their jobs. They placed John in solitary confinement. I will let him out today."

Trial 23

I must let John out today for my own sake. Not being able to read his journal last night had irritated me to no end. I am deeply invested in his story.

"Oh," Dr. Mandalay said, "good. I'm glad. Still, I think we should tell him what we're doing. It could strengthen his resolve and make it easier for him to regain his memories."

I told her, "No. He must be ignorant. He must find the path to his memories himself."

I could hardly believe Mandalay's stupidity. If John knew he was an experiment, the process would be ruined. John would rebel. She should have known that. We have been enough of these trials to know better. Besides, this is a two-way experiment. Both applications MUST be tested.

"I can't stand to watch another patient go insane and kill themselves," she said. And then I saw it, her moral corruption. After so many trials, Mandalay's supple heart has grown weak. Her conscience has finally collapsed. Like always, Mandalay has let her emotions confuse her. I could see it in her jitteriness, her unsure eyes. Had she started seeing a psychiatrist again? Perhaps Dr. Mandalay needs a trial of her own. Her and the eggheads.

"John is strong," I said. I had to put her at ease, stop her before she did something rash. "I will release him from the lower cells today and continue the procedure. He is at a point now where his inner mind is projecting over the outer world. He must be allowed to move freely through it. If all goes well, John will regain his memories and the ability to project his thoughts will be forever his. He will be a god among men."

"And if he kills again?"

"I would sacrifice every patient in this building to see our dream realized, Margaret. Would you not?"

She squirmed, nervous. Mandalay's kind heart will be the death of her. "No," she said. "I can't handle it. I can't take the violence."

"I see." I placed my cigar in its ashtray, folded my arms and laid a stern gaze on Mandalay. "You must stay strong for me just a little while longer. John is the last, I promise. Help me see it through to the end with John and I will allow you to resign."

A lie, of course. If Mandalay thinks she can walk away from Wentworth, she will find herself spending the rest of her life in a cell.

"You mean it?" Her eyes gleamed at the prospect of leaving.

"Yes, now go away. I must summon John and put his mind at ease."

Mandalay left, giddy at the

Trial 23

thought of distancing herself from our work, the work we have struggled so hard to perfect. Daft woman. I will see to her after John's trials are complete. Perhaps before. Margaret Mandalay has outgrown her purpose here. There is no room for doubt in my hospital.

The date is October 27th

I stand in the face of a great conspiracy. Mr. Strong and Mr. Clean came for me this morning, liberated me from my dungeon asylum. I was surprised to say the least. I had thought I would rot down there. I was prepared to lose my mind and become an animal. But the bald bastards came and escorted me to Windhelm's office. "Don't kill anyone today," Mr. Clean told me in the elevator. Nasally fuck. And his gangly partner snickered.

In Windhelm's office, I took a seat and there was an awkward moment of silence, surely on purpose. Doctor Windhelm loves to watch me squirm. And squirm I did. I was afraid he would sentence me to life in Wentworth Psychiatric Hospital for what I had done, for the violence I had unleashed on the sad and unfortunate Mr. Bernie.

"Bernie," the doctor said, sucking on his cigar. "Bernie killed himself. Tragic, really. He committed suicide with his fists. Horrific, in fact. He beat himself to death. Rather ugly."

I stared, totally in shock. Windhelm was telling me that Bernie had bashed his own skull into fragments. What kind of game was he playing?

"Yes, I'm afraid Bernie was unstable. It was only a matter of time before something like this happened. You will be returned to your normal cell, number 244. We will continue the fight to recover your memories. Do not stress, dear boy. You have done no wrong."

Trial 23

He was up to something. Windhelm knew damn well I had stomped Bernie to death. I remembered it vividly. I had snapped out of the dream just as I was being dragged off by the orderlies. I still remember Bernie's trampled head. "You're sure?" I asked.

"Quite sure. There is no one to blame but Bernie. A misunderstanding is all. I will have your journal brought to your normal cell and I will see to it that you are fed like a king this afternoon. Cheeseburgers perhaps, for your trouble."

"A cheeseburger would be great." I didn't know what else to say. I wasn't about to argue with the good doctor, insist it was I who killed ol' Bernie. That seemed counterproductive. Better to let him play his game.

"Excellent." He folded his hands, looked through his shroud of smoke at me. "We understand each other, correct?"

"We do." I did not know why, but Windhelm was offering me a get of jail free card. I took it. I was not about to spend another night in the dank underground prison if I didn't need to. "Thank you," I said. Then, kind of reluctantly, "You're sure I'm not crazy? Because I really, really feel like I'm going crazy."

"Quite sure." He made a face, sighed and said, "John, sometimes with amnesia, the brain tries to compensate for its missing memories. This can manifest in different ways. Confusion, hallucinations, hearing voices. It is not uncommon for someone suffering from brain trauma to feel incomplete, or perhaps insane. Yet it is only the shattered mind trying to restructure itself, to fill in the gaps. This sometimes results in visual and audio irregularities."

That was when I realized Windhelm had been reading my journal. Sneaky fucker. He knew I was having graphic hallucinations. He was trying to dismiss them as normal. But why? To keep me docile? Calm? Manageable?

"The brain is a powerful organ, John. The brain is the true god, capable of miracles. When there is something the brain cannot understand, sometimes it will try to make sense of it in a unique way, creating its own fantasies to fill in the blanks. This may come in the form of delusional episodes. These episodes may be triggered by stress, anxiety, a flare of emotion."

I cocked my eyebrow. Now that he said it, I realized each of my inexplicable experiences had come right after a surge of anxiety: In the M.R.I machine when I was having a panic attack. The first night I slept in my cell. When I was uncomfortable eating with the other nutcases in the cafeteria. After Windhelm upset me in his office. After I killed a man.

He said, "Your brain is full of holes, John. It may be trying to fill them. I assure you there is nothing to worry about. Your sanity is indeed intact. You suffer only from amnesia."

It was a hell of an explanation. Crazy enough to believe. My brain got rattled and broke, began to generate imagery based on my buried memories, some fucked up superpower. A lot better than being insane and delusional. Still, it was almost too believable, too convenient. I was sure Windhelm was manipulating me. But why? Why placate me? Why buy my appeasement with cheeseburgers? I couldn't figure it out. I couldn't decide whether I was insane, whether I had amnesia, or whether I was a messy jumble of both. It hurt my mind. So much thinking, so many contradictory feelings, so much fucking uncertainty!

I left Windhelm's office confused, just wanting to remember my damn past. It's the only way to be certain about anything, about who I am, about what really

Trial 23

brought me to Wentworth. A car accident? Still sounds fishy to me, too fucking easy.

It dawned on me then, as I followed Mr. Strong through the empty maze of hallways, that to rediscover who I am, I must embrace my illusions. I must delve deeper. The key to remembering who I am is buried somewhere in the dreamscape. I'm sure of it. There must be an end, albeit likely terrifying. And at that end is me, flayed open in all my hideous glory.

That was when it happened. My confusion, my paranoia, my deep contemplation—it opened a portal to the shadow dimension.

We had been going along past the billions of closed doors in stark silence, Mr. Clean plodding behind me and Mr. Strong leading the way. Then an office door was flung open and a parade of kids spilled into the hallway. Ravers, glow sticks around their necks, dilated pupils, neon shirts. They bumped into me, somehow multiplying until the whole corridor was full of raving lunatics partying to the loud boom of electronic dance music. It was like trying to swim upstream, trying to maneuver through the swarm of drunks. I soon lost sight of Mr. Strong and Mr. Clean. The animals had clogged the hallway. Then came the strobes, flashing green and red lights. Artificial smoke hissed around my feet and wafted into my face. All I could see were flashing colors and blocky shapes. I waved away the smoke, coughed, and pushed my way through the throng of sweaty party animals to a table at the edge of the bar.

They were as nuts as the droolers in Wentworth. Fucking kids, young people having fun beneath the oscillating spotlights. Writhing, grinding, tongues slithering into mouths. Topless women, dudes with sunglasses on. This, I thought, was the real madhouse. The fanatics pounded their fists, gave hails to their machine god.

I very abruptly needed a drink. I left my table and struggled through the animals. Real animals. Dissolution in their eyes, total insanity. They convulsed to the electronic rabble and computerized warbles, spasming beneath the hectic light. Primal, ritualistic heathens. They frothed, sweat, danced. I heard their voices. "Graog, graog," they said, absolute nothing in their black eyes. Horny insects in their hive.

"What'll you have, pal?" the bartender asked me. He was all wit and teeth, a dapper man in a bowler hat, a red and black checkered suit with a charcoal tie like a fucking blackjack dealer.

"Whiskey," I said. It felt appropriate.

"Coming up." He poured me a whiskey and added ice from a bucket under the counter, the long plank of booze-soaked wood where the thirsty animals were lined up to drowned. Passing it to me he said, "On the house, champ. Drink up. Forget your worries."

"Thanks." I slugged it back. "I'll have another." And he filled my glass. "What is this place?"

"This is Jack's place. I'm Jack, friend. Pleasure's mine. Have a smoke." He slid a pack of cigarettes across to me, a lighter too. I sparked a cigarette and leaned against the bar, already feeling fuzzy in my head.

"Someone was killed in front of your place," I said. "You have a monster in your basement." It seemed normal enough, a fine thing to say in such a wild place. I kind of liked it in there, watching the anarchy, the animals fucking on the dancefloor.

"Don't think about it," he said. Jack was sharp, I could tell. A real pusher. Charismatic, intelligent, something nefarious cooking behind his eyes. "Finish your drink, friend. Forget your worries."

"I killed him," I said. "It was me." I took a sip of whiskey, winced, wiped my mouth. "He was waiting

Trial 23

for me but I never showed. He got gunned down, robbed, killed by a freak. He was waiting for me."

"Put it aside," Jack said. "Leave the past to rot. Have a drink. Forget all about it."

I snuffed out my cigarette, finished the last bit of whiskey in my glass. "Maybe you're right," I said. "I'll have another drink."

My glass was already full. Jack leaned on the counter and winked at me, wicked the way he looked, his stupid bowler hat. "That's the spirit, friend. Kill the memory. Drink and forget."

I was already forgetful. Two glasses of whiskey had me feeling good, feeling numb. I sucked the third one back, greedy to get drunk and settle into a comfortable fugue.

Some asshole bumped into me, stuttered in his insect language, "Srrry bugho. Tornu gettt a burzzzz." His eyes black, too big for his head. Something fluttered under his shirt.

I watched him slink down the bar, and that was when I saw her, a lone woman on a barstool, more beautiful than words can describe. She wore a scarlet dress, had pale skin and silky black hair. A moon baby, perfect and entrancing. She was a goddess. A fucking goddess. I drank her in, her radiance, her curves, her utter perfection.

"Who is that?" I asked Jack.

He glanced, made a face like he had seen a cockroach. "No one, man. She's not for you. Don't pay too close attention. Have another drink."

"No, I want to see her." I was fixated, completely in love. Her scarlet wrapped skin, her lines. She was magical.

But Jack thumped the bottle of whiskey onto the counter and distracted me. "You don't even need a glass. Drink the bottle, pal. Have your fill."

And when I looked back she had been

swallowed by the swarm, a dozen men with huge insect eyes buzzing around her, their shirts fluttering, twitching. I felt the need to save her. I got off the barstool and took a step. Drunk, my guts lurched and I stopped. "Toilet. Jack, where's the toilet?"

"That way, friend." He gestured to the back of the room, the dingy corridor to the toilets.

I looked back down the bar and the goddess was gone, pulled into the hive, into the insect chatter. Knowing she was gone gave me a cramp. I wanted to see her face again, to see her alone at the bar, beautiful and compelling. She had looked to be waiting for someone. I was sorry to go, but I was about to be sick. I clutched my belly as I waddled through the writhing mass and into the toilet.

Vomit, a lot of it. I puked Jack's whiskey into the toilet until I wept and my throat was sore, the taste of bile making me even sicker. I sounded like a dying animal inside the stall.

Within minutes I was out of barf. I felt better. My buzz was gone. I collected myself from the piss-stained floor and exited the stall, came to linger in the empty bathroom.

Lights flickered, mirrors dusty above the cracked porcelain sinks. Their black glass looked like dead portals to other worlds. I went to wash my hands, staring into one of the dead mirrors as muddy water was spat between my fingers. The mirror came to life. It warbled, became clear, and I was looking through a window at a terrible beast.

He was a white ogre, this thing staring at me in the mirror. Though it was more like staring at me through a window. Wherever the monster was it looked cold, his breath exhaled in tufts of white. He leered at me with magma eyes, his skull enormous, white and powdery. An evil abomination, hairless with huge pale muscles. He mimicked my movement as if a reflection of myself. I shifted left, the beast shifted with me. I blinked, the beast blinked. I took a step backwards, so did he, more of his grossly muscular body showing through the window.

I moved in close, our faces nearly touching. *What?* I mouthed, and so did he. I could almost taste the chill behind the mirror. Then he smashed his fists against the glass and scared the shit out of me. I jumped. "What the fuck!" And he continued to beat on the glass with his huge white fists. He bawled, but I couldn't hear it. He beat on the glass until it cracked and his image corrupted and he was gone, the mirror fractured in a hundred places.

If only it had stayed that way. The broken glass took on a glow, dull at first but it intensified. It became rosy, then fierce red. Fire, I thought. A fire raged behind the glass. The woman's body smashed through it so fast I leapt back screaming and landed on my ass.

It was like she had crashed through a windshield. The woman from the bar broke halfway through the mirror but got stuck on the glass; it dug into her stomach, made her bleed, the blood weeping into the sink beneath her. She tried to push herself through, pressed off the glass with her hands and grunted. But she was stuck, trapped half in the bathroom and the half in a world of fire, redness flaring behind her. It appeared to be cooking her legs.

"My god!" I scrambled up. Her scarlet dress was shredded, blood frothing from her mouth as she coughed. Such a beautiful thing in so much pain. "Let me help." I took her arms and pulled, but the shards of glass cut her deeply and she moaned.

"No, leave me. Run from this place."

"Not without you." I was panicked. For a reason beyond my understanding, I was drawn to this woman. She possessed me. I needed to save her, to make her pain go away. "What happened to you? How can I help?"

"Remember me," she said. "For once in your miserable life, do what I ask and remember me."

I gaped, feeling helpless. The fire raged behind the glass. The sink was filling with blood. She was going pale, deathly white as her life faded. "I don't know who you are," I said. "Please tell me. At least your name. Do you know my name?"

"Sweet hollow." She touched my cheek, her skin cold yet soothing. "Don't fall into the darkness. Don't forget me."

The fire consumed her. I watched in horror as she was burned alive. She arced and screamed, body aflame, and crumbled to ash just like the boy in the room had. Her ashes floated listlessly through the darkened bathroom like fallout. The fire died behind the glass, mirror shattered into a thousand fragments. And me, alone in the darkness, feeling wretched, like I had just witnessed my guardian angel scorched alive by hellfire.

Then every light flickered on above the remaining mirrors. **Remember** was written across their glass in red lipstick. But only for a second. The lights flicked and went dim and written in black paint was the word **forget**, center of every mirror.

I blinked, licked my lips, and turned to walk out of the bathroom. It was too much. Something important had just happened. Between the woman stuck in the mirror, the pale beast in its cold lair, and forces beyond my understanding urging me to either forget or remember, there was a vital message to decode. Unfortunately, it sifted through the bottom of my mind before I could even touch it.

Trial 23

The bar was closed, dark except for the lights above Jack's bar. The handsome barman sat on a stool, smoked, drank. He smiled when he saw me, tilted his stupid hat. "Welcome back, friend. They've gone home for the night, filthy animals."

My footsteps echoed over the hollow dancefloor as I made my way to him. It smelt like sweat and semen, a thin layer of alcohol. The floor was covered in spit and plastic cups.

Jack passed me a drink as I sat down. "For your sorrows, dear boy."

I looked at the rusty liquid in the glass, not really wanting it, yet at the same time wanting it more than anything. I took one very careful sip, then pushed the glass away. "Maybe next time," I said. "Tell me where the girl went."

Jack acted dumb. "What girl?"

"The one I noticed earlier. You saw her. She had a red dress, black hair, beautiful beyond description. Did she…" I hesitated. "Did she drive home with someone?"

Jack scrunched his face. "Forget her, man. There are a million girls out in the world, thousands of wet panties for you to sniff. Forget about that one, huh. Have a drink. I'll fix you up something real nice. House special."

"What was her name?"

"Not important." Jack climbed over the bar, grabbed bottles and began to mix me a rather toxic-looking drink. "She's nothing. She's no one. Some street walker. Takes john's out back and tugs them off for a buck."

I shook my head. "No, that doesn't feel right. I can almost say her name. It starts with an M, I think. The letters are right on the tip of my tongue."

Jack's eyes got real big. "Drink this." He shoved a drink in my face, a blue cocktail with a red finish. "It's the house special. It's Jack's special. Have a slurp." He was impatient, grinning nervously. "Just have a taste, friend. You'll love it."

I took the drink. "You have to tell me her name," I said. "I'll drink it if you tell me her name."

"Whatever." Jack beamed. "Just drink it, friend. No worries, no hassle. Forget about it."

It smelt good, like sweet apples. I drank the whole thing in four gulps and tipped off my stool, hit the ground hard with my shoulder. Vision blurry, I saw Jack grinning above me. "Time to sleep," he said. "Into dreamland, friend, the land of forgetfulness."

I passed out. Jack had poisoned me.

There was a homestyle bacon cheeseburger wrapped in tinfoil when I snapped back into reality. It was on the table in front of me, smelling delicious, looking so damn scrumptious. It was lunchtime and I was in the cafeteria at my usual spot, the crazy-eyed old man ogling me across the table and chewing on his mustache hairs. It disturbed me that I was getting used to him. More disturbing was when I realized I had been out for four straight hours! The last thing I remembered was walking down the hall from Windhelm's office. That had been before breakfast.

I looked around. No one was dead. I had no blood on my knuckles. Mr. Strong and Mr. Clean stood by the doorway with their arms folded, looking like a pair of eunuch bouncers. Ugly warts. They paid me no mind. No one did. I was astounded to have lasted four hours in a fugue without causing at least some sort of damage. Was I gaining control?

Greedily, I scarfed down my burger. There was still a vomity aftertaste in my mouth and the burger's deliciousness got rid of it. As I ate, I thought about Jack, the mad proprietor of his filthy bar. He was a deceptive

Trial 23

bastard, no doubt about it. He had tried to drown me with booze, had poisoned me so I wouldn't ask questions about the girl. M-somebody. I could almost remember her name. It was so close. She felt important, like someone I wasn't supposed to forget. I thought she had come to guide me through my horrors, or at least try. She had failed, been roasted alive. The memory of her cooked flesh soured the last few bites of my burger.

Lunch finished and I was taken to my room. My original room. My box of blinding light. Mr. Clean and Mr. Strong were oddly passive, saying nothing to me and gently closing the door once I was inside. "Have a nice day, kid," Mr. Clean said. I wondered what had gotten into them. The eggheads were acting as if they had been reprimanded, bent over Windhelm's knee and given spankings. I would have loved to see that, the two bald creeps bent over the savage doctor's knee, wailing like oversized babies as he wailed on their asses.

I'm going to picture it now as I fall asleep. Well, I'm going to try. It's hard to picture anything other than her face, her eyes, her ebony hair, her red dress. Fantasy or not, she's all I can think about.

Boris Chapman's personal log: October 27/10

That little prick. What the fuck is Windhelm feeding him? What's he got in those white pills? The son of a bitch stopped halfway down the hall and yacked all over the floor, chunky green puke shit out of his mouth. Fuck that, I ain't a janitor. We left the puke on the floor and took Windhelm's boy for breakfast in the cafeteria.

Normally, Edgar and I would have kicked the shit out of a patient for pulling a dumbass stunt like puking on the floor. But Windhelm had a cute meeting with us this morning, a little fucking parlay. He was concerned about our behavior, said we'd been neglecting our duties. Fucking quack. He doesn't know the half of it. Still, he told us to hike up our socks or we're gone, done, fired. It must have something to do with his patient. Or maybe Dug opened his filthy fucking mouth. Either way, Edgar and I aren't stupid. You don't get fired from Wentworth. You get repurposed, and I don't feel like being the doctor's next experiment.

So yeah, we were nice to the kid. I didn't say shit about his batty fucking eyes, all crystally and weird like he had shards of glass in his retinas. Almost reminded me of someone high on speed. It was fucked up. He ate his food and came with us to his cell, totally coherent, but something altogether different was going on in his eyes. He was fucking

Trial 23

vacant. It lasted for hours. He was blitzed all the way till lunch. Not until we got that cheeseburger under his nose did he snap out of it.

Whatever Windhelm's done to "perfect" his procedure seems to be working, even with our interference. His boy's still alive, slipping in and out of crazy, killing motherfuckers one day and eating cheeseburgers the next. The kid's got free roam of the hospital, total fucking immunity. I don't even pretend to know what's going on or why he's so important. All I know is Windhelm made a grave fucking error this morning when he threatened to fire us. Don't ever threaten me, little bitch. Your days are done.

Edgar and I fashioned ourselves a plan. We're not about to be "fired." Fuck that. You won't catch me swallowing one of Doc's poisons, inhaling one of his psychoactive gases. I've seen the shit in his lab. I know all the tricky ways he has of getting his secret serum inside you. Shit, I've helped him pump it into half our damn patients. How else would they have gotten so fucking crazy? Anyway, it sure as shit ain't getting inside me or Edgar. This place will burn before that happens. Windhelm's finished. Quack motherfucker.

October 28th.

With rest came clarity. I lay in bed a long time last night thinking, ruminating, cycling the facts through my head. I couldn't sleep. It was obvious Windhelm had lied to me. No way could stress have induced my four-hour blackout. It was not my brain regenerating, creating its own memories. Not a chance. It was something deeper, biological, psychoactive. Windhelm's somehow altered my brain, manipulated it, then tried to cover it up with pseudo-science. I'm not crazy. I'm not delusional. Windhelm's a goddamn mad scientist. He's been working me like a puppet. The only question is how! And why?

My thoughts then shifted to the dreamworld itself, the magical realm the good doctor has sucked me into. It's all connected. Everything, the whole sick show. Jack, the Eater, the guy in the denim jacket, the little girl and the raven monster, the cinder man, the burnt angel. They're all players, actors on an elaborate stage, my own perverse universe come to life.

But I'll be damned if I can make sense of it. There are still pieces missing, fragmented, scattered throughout my mind. The story is told in tricks and metaphors, disguises and subtle clues, fucking subliminal advertising. I can't figure out the plot, the scheme, the goddamn characters. It's convoluted and vague. A beautiful woman and a pale giant; a crazed bartender; a disturbed family; unnatural monsters in lairs and labs. It's a fucking freakshow. I guess that makes me the blind ringmaster. After all, it is my story. It's my damn story and I'm lost in it.

Even after I slipped into another terror last night in my sleep, another obscure chapter of what I am coming to realize is my life, I am still no closer to decoding the enigma of who I am. I still do not have a clear vision of my past.

The smell of smoke stirred me from sleep. I woke on a couch, on a badly burned sofa in the middle of a badly burned room. The fire was long dead, but it still stank like smoke. The apartment was beyond repair, everything consumed, destroyed.

I was in the living room. A television set sat in a pile of cold cinders and ash, its screen shattered. Soot covered the floor, the ceiling scorched and black. The entire place had been ravaged by flame. It was a disaster.

Getting up, I moved from the ruined couch and into the kitchen. The countertops were stained by the fire, cupboards half eaten. The refrigerator's shell had bubbled from the heat, yet somehow a picture remained taped to its door. In the picture was the woman from the bar, M-somebody. I had to take a second to admire her, beautiful at the beach in a red bikini. Smiling, radiant. Someone had their arm wrapped around her but their face was burnt from the photo. Some guy. Lucky prick.

Curious, I opened the fridge and found dozens upon dozens of crinkled black beer cans. The fridge was stocked with them. "Huh." I closed the door. Whoever had lived in the apartment was clearly an alcoholic.

Standing then in the silence of devastation it was hard to escape the crushing sense of loss, of overwhelming grief. A great calamity had taken place right where I stood. I felt it in my bones, deep in my soul. I was lingering in the ruins of a person's home, in the burned and sooty remains of a life. It shamed me in a way. I felt desolate, as sad and empty and broken as the apartment.

Then came a scratching noise from down the hall as if someone was trying to claw their way out of a coffin, the distinct scratch of fingernails against wood. I followed it, feet sifting through the ash and rubble of the kitchen, into the hallway, which was even more damaged than the rest. The wallpaper was completely gone, huge claw marks in the blackened wood as if a bear had marked the walls in a mad rampage.

I paused to look into an open doorway, to regard the vacant space inside. Nothingness, a gulf I could barely fathom, the entire room scrubbed from existence.

I kept on past the burnt-out husk of a washroom and arrived at the end of the hall, came into the threshold of the final room. It was the origin of the scratching noise.

Someone was locked in a closet. They tried furiously to claw their way out, door rattling like crazy. I thought about helping whoever it was to escape, but the room frightened me terribly. It was only a bit burnt, the slightly charred master bedroom. But it provoked a feeling of dread in me and I refused to enter. I hated the cute paintings on the walls, the sensible decor, the jewelry boxes on the dresser. The normalcy of it made my skin crawl. Then there was the pocket of blackness beneath the bed. It was a black hole, a fucking pit to Hell. And from it came a deep rumble.

The scratching stopped. I held my breath. The whole damn room quaked. Seconds later and a pair of massive golden talons emerged from the darkness below the bed, dug into the floorboards and shot splinters into my face. I staggered backwards into the hall, aghast at the monster rising from its pit, its huge shoulders

Trial 23

ripping the bed in half. It was hideous, an amalgamation of horror. And in seconds it loomed above me.

SHE. The horror was a she. She broke through the doorway and I fell on my ass, scuttled back against the wall of the hallway and gaped at the monstrosity. Her forearms were armored with black steel like the gauntlets of a demon knight, ending in a trio of brutal gold talons. She was built to kill, yet was so much more, part dead, part woman, all ghoulishly malformed. Molted red cloth was stitched across her breasts and groin with steel wire, her exposed flesh decomposed, bruised like a spoiled banana. She had no face, only a veil of ebony hair that wound around her neck like a noose. And she had no stomach. There was a square hollow between her cloth-wrapped breasts and groin, two thin strips of carrion flesh on the sides. Sprouted from each of the four sides were rotted baby arms, little hands gripping the handles of a treasure chest. Intricately carved, plated gold, the chest jittered as the woman stepped forward, the baby arms wiggling like springs. One even adjusted its grip.

It was the first time I shrieked so stringently in the dreamworld. Really shrieked, out of sheer terror. The woman frightened me beyond rationale. I crawled from her on my hands and knees, floundered to my feet and sprinted down the hall. Her steps rocked the apartment as she gave chase. Soot rained from the ceiling.

I made it to the living room, vaulted over the couch and hit a dead end. There was no door, just a wall. I pressed my back against it, quivering with a knot in my throat as the woman roared towards me, the reassembled deformity of dead flesh. I cringed, held perfectly still—

A crash from the end of the hall, a quick pitter-patter of steps. The monster was nearly upon me. I could see the designs on the box as it wobbled in her hollow, see the green rot on the babies' fingernails. Then came Jack. He shoved the woman aside and pivoted around her, slammed into me and screamed in my face, "Why are you here? Are you fucking crazy, man? You'll die here!" He looked insane, frazzled. His fingernails were chipped and bloody.

I had no words. So much was happening. Jack pulled a silver drink mixer from his suit and gave it a quick shake. "You've got to get away from her, friend. She'll be the death of you." I could smell the sweet apple of his poison. "You have wandered too far." Mixing desperately. "Quick, drink this." He shoved the mixer under my nose and tilted it, and I drank, not even thinking. I just wanted to be away from the roasted apartment, from the faceless she-beast.

"Good boy," he said. "Sleep now. Forget." He gave a sigh of relief just as the monster punched through the center of Jack's face, three golden points exiting his eyes and mouth like she wanted to bowl with his head. She closed her fist and Jack's face imploded, his features sucked inwards in a wash of blood and eye and teeth.

And then I was out. The world darkened and I was gone.

I woke sitting on the edge of my bed, fully aware as if I had been awake for the last hour. I heard a loud bang and looked at the door, thought someone had just closed it. Was someone in my room?

Trial 23

Margaret's Journal: 10/28/10

I read John's journal. Windhelm left me no choice. Poor John was throwing up in the halls. I peeked into the cafeteria yesterday and saw him zombified, his eyes glossed over, staring off into space. I went early this morning to John's cell, secretly without Windhelm's permission, and was not surprised to find him in much the same state, catatonic behind his eyes yet coherent when I spoke to him. It's clear to me that John has retreated into his mind, the strange world he has created. What's left is no more than a stupid shell, a mindless drone. I fear the worst.

    I didn't need to do much, just asked John to wait in the hallway and I sat on his bed and read the entirety of his journal. It took about an hour. John was still brainwashed when I invited him back into his cell. His face was vacant, but something intense was going on inside his head. I swear I could see sparks in his eyes, flares of emotion. But the poor boy was null. I fear it's only a matter of time before he gets stuck in the dark fantasy of his past, or before one of his ghoulish manifestations kills him. If John dies in his alternate reality, I am confident he will die in real life.

    The fact remains, the procedure is not going as Windhelm claimed it to be. John is not projecting his thoughts outwards. He's trapped in a grim dimension of skewed memories. The trauma of his past is too severe. Even with the formula, poor John can't reconcile what's happened to him. Instead, he's manifested bizarre creatures to symbolize his guilt, his fear, the tormentors of his life. The whole point of the procedure was to unlock John's mind, give him free roam of his past. It's why an amnesiac makes such an interesting test subject. Once John gained control of his thoughts and emotions, he was supposed to be able to overlap them with reality, make a kind of hologram for himself.

Clearly, that's not happening. John's too corrupt. The procedure is flawed. His memories have mutated into something dangerous, and now he's gradually being locked inside the scary world of his past. Poor boy. He's on the brink of insanity. He's one bad trip away from death. Windhelm lied to me. He's not healing John. He's making him go crazy. But why? When did the doctor become so wicked?

The worst of it is that John knows. He's figured it out. At first he thought he was delusional, a very real patient of the hospital. And who could blame him? But he's a smart boy. He's figured it out. John knows Windhelm has manipulated him, somehow encouraged his visions. What John doesn't know is how or why. How could he? John can't even clue together the pieces of his dreams to understand who he is. And soon he'll be catatonic, stuck in a never-ending nightmare. Or worse, one of his manifestations will kill him, or he will stray off the path and fall into the blackness that encroaches at the corners of his hallucinations.

Poor boy. It's up to me to get John out, away from the hospital and ween the drugs out of his system, try to cleanse him of Windhelm's toxins. Perhaps I will do it tonight when the hospital is dark and the goons have gone home. It's only noon. There's still time to save John.

My therapist told me to take charge. She said I need to impose some authority in my life, that it'll help me

Trial 23

overcome my anxiety and squeamishness. After reading John's journal, I went to my office and dug out all the files on our other patients, poor 7047 who killed herself and the others who died after botched procedures and the rest abandoned in the bowels of this hospital. I collected all the notes on our formula. I've got it all, enough evidence to condemn Windhelm to life in prison and shut down Wentworth for good. And unfortunately, to incriminate myself as well. Though perhaps I deserve to be behind bars. Either way, I have the proof in my satchel. All there is to do is steal John under the cover of night, get him in my car and drive away. I warned the doctor. I told him I won't watch anyone else die. I was serious.

Once I get John out, I'll go to the press, the police. I'll tell the whole world about the sick things we've done here.

October 28th.

More riddles. Endless. None of it makes sense. I went from the charred remains of an apartment to a graveyard at the edge of the abyss. I'm starting to wonder if I'm dead. Am I reliving my life and seeing the true horror of it? Is this my divine punishment for… what? Was I a bad father? Was I a demon in a man's mask? Was I the embodiment of fear, a grey worm of a creature who feasted on the fears of others? Was that how I got off? Did I burn my apartment? Did I… Oh god. Did I run over the black-haired beauty in my car? Is that how I ended up at Wentworth?

    I hadn't considered it until now, but perhaps I've been looking at things from the wrong perspective. Maybe it's me who's my own worst nightmare, the plague of my life, the poisonous bane of my existence. Me all along! What if I'm being tormented by the hideous truth of who I used to be? What if the monsters I've battled are shadows of my former self, ugly abominations of the man I once I was?

    Oh god, I'm spiraling again. I should write down the second phase of today's events before I tear out my hair in frustration. It could be that I missed something vital.

I started sweating during breakfast, profuse fat-guy sweat. It was so bad I had to ask Mr. Clean and Mr. Strong to take me to the showers. "I need it," I told them. "Please,

Trial 23

I'm sweating like a son of a bitch. I just need to cool off."

"Sure," Mr. Strong said. I thought it was weird that he agreed so easily, weirder still when him and his ogre of a partner exchanged evil grins. "Let's go. Shower all you want, kid. Fuck it."

We went from the cafeteria to the showers, me tugging on my collar the whole way. I was burning up, but it wasn't a fever. I was just hot, moist, oozing sweat.

There was no one else in the showers so early in the morning. The eggheads hung back at the entrance like my personal bodyguards while I stripped naked and turned the cold water on full blast. I stood beneath the rain with my head down, relieved to cool off. I shut my eyes and enjoyed it, the bitter cold. It crept into my bones, prickled my skin. I started to shiver, and that was when I realized the water had stopped. But it was still freezing cold. I opened my eyes and it was dark, a deep chill in the air.

And the air was stuffy. I felt claustrophobic. I couldn't see. I reached out and touched a wall of stone six inches from me, chipped and rough like the wall of a cave. Then it hit me. I was entombed!

"Let me out!" I banged on the wall. "Someone let me out of here!" I was in a damned sarcophagus. "Help me!"

Someone was scuffling around outside mumbling to themselves. I couldn't make out their words through the stone. My tomb rocked as they hit it with something. There was a loud crack, a sliver of light as the lid to my coffin was slowly pried open. Whoever was outside gave a grunt, the lid sliding inch by inch to reveal moonlight, to reveal Jack the bartender with his shoulder against the lid, struggling to push the damn thing off.

"Come on, you fuck." With one final grunt, Jack shouldered the heavy lid off and it crashed to the ground, crumbled to pieces. I immediately leapt out, sucked in a huff of fresh air while Jack leaned against the shell of my tomb and panted. "Too many cigarettes, friend. I'm damn exhausted." As he pulled a pack of cigarettes from his checkered suit and lit one. "But I need it, you know. Sweet addiction."

I should have known the treacherous bastard was still alive. "What are you doing here?" I asked. "I thought your head imploded."

"Just a flesh wound, friend. Nothing to worry about. In fact, you're best to forget you were ever in that burned-out shithole. Best to forget about the woman, too. She'll claw your face off, leave you shredded."

Hard to tell Jack's truth from lies. I had a feeling there was a bit of both in everything he said. And yet I was deathly terrified of the she-beast, the perfect incarnation of horror. I had no doubt she would tear me to shreds. I wondered if she had destroyed the Eater, the demon, just to sink her claws into me herself.

"What is this place?" I asked. It looked like a family crypt. There was the large tomb Jack had busted me out of, a slightly smaller one beside it, and a tiny baby-sized sarcophagus beside that. They could have fit inside each other like Russian dolls.

"It's nowhere, friend. In fact, we ought to split. The sooner the better. She's apt to catch your scent, could come storming out of the woods at any minute and claw both our guts out. Not to mention the others, eh, the creeps who haunt this place and lurk through the forbidden crypts. No, man. We should split, get ourselves a drink."

"I don't want a drink." It felt weird to say, but it was true. Booze seemed unimportant. I was more fascinated by the angel statue at the head of the open-air crypt, her benevolent face looking at the moon,

Trial 23

swaddling a small babe in her arms like the baby Jesus. I thought she looked like the M-woman cast in stone.

"Sure you do," Jack said. "Since when do you refuse a drink? What, you'd rather stay in this forgotten place with the spooks and the specters? Have you gone nuts?"

I ignored Jack. He was an annoying chirp in my ear. Besides, I was busy admiring the statue, positive it was the black-haired woman from Jack's bar, the one who had crashed through the mirror and told me to remember, the one I couldn't get out of my head. "Who is she?" I asked, caressing the stone baby in her arms, surprised to find it warm to touch. "Is she the one entombed beside me? Is that her baby in the small coffin?"

"Man, are you deaf?" Jack tried to pull me from the statue. "You'll die here. We've got to go. Forget about her. Stop asking questions."

I wriggled free of Jack's grip. "Just tell me her name. What's your problem?"

"I told you before," he said, sighing impatiently. "She's just a whore, a two-bit hooker. Forget about her and come with me. Look, my place is just outside." He pointed through the doorway of the crypt, at the big neon sign for Jack's bar flashing on the crest of a foggy hill in the distance, a thin dirt track winding to it through countless rows of headstones. "I can guide you through the graveyard safely," he said. "We can take shelter at my place, drink ourselves into oblivion."

"I don't want to," I said. "I'm tired of forgetting. I want to remember. Damnit, Jack, tell me her name." I whirled and picked up the prybar Jack had used to break me out of my tomb. "Or else I'll open these coffins and see for myself who's inside."

"No!" Jack reached, tried to steal the prybar from my hands. "Don't open those, friend. They're sealed for a reason. Leave the dead to rot."

We fought and it got heated, a desperate tug-o-war for the prybar. I waited for Jack to pull as hard as he could, then used his own leverage against him and smashed the prybar into his forehead, knocking off his stupid bowler hat, knocking Jack flat on his ass.

"Don't do it," he said. "You don't know what's in there."

But I already had the bar jammed in the crevice of the woman-sized coffin. I pushed so hard my eyeballs hurt. The coffin cracked, and with one desperate push the lid toppled over and broke into fragments. The tomb was unsealed, but there was nothing in it, a deep and dark hole like some bottomless pit. "Nothing," I said, "it's empty."

Jack moved so quick I almost didn't see him. He sprang to his feet and launched himself at me, hands outstretched to shove me through the coffin and into the nothingness.

I pivoted just in time, swung wide with the curved end of the prybar and gouged out a chunk of Jack's head. The force of it sent him stumbling towards the open coffin, but he caught himself on its edges before he could be sucked in. He looked at me. "I just wanted to—" And I swung again and broke Jack's cheekbone with a dense thud.

Now he was limp, barely able to stand, sagging in the mouth of the coffin. "I was only protecting you," he said. "I was saving you from yourself. It's better to forget, friend. The truth will kill you."

I sneered at him, the lying fuck. Jack's cheek was red and swollen. It burst like a zit when I smacked it again with the prybar, blood spraying me in the face. "I want to remember," I yelled at him. "I don't want to forget."

His eyelids fluttered. "You'll die here without me…" And all I had to do was give him a little push.

Trial 23

"Goodbye, Jack." And he fell backwards into the coffin's spooky portal. Jack faded away like a bad mirage.

I didn't have the stomach to touch the infant's sarcophagus. Something about it unnerved me, as though if I touched it I'd be desecrating something holy. I let it be and abandoned the crypt, giving the statue of the angelic woman and her sweet infant a last sad look before I left.

My crypt was one of many a top a hill, dozens upon dozens of crude mausoleums built over each other like the ruins of an ancient city. Statues of men, of women, of darker demons rose ugly between the stone complexes, ungodly monuments to the deceased. The dead were restless in the graveyard. Chilling wails drifted on the fog and peculiar shadows moved in and out of the crypts like timid goblins. I thought about what Jack had said, about the spooks and the specters, and put my feet to work.

There was a trail leading down the slope, winding through fields of tombstones and bony trees to the border of an immense and impossibly dark forest. I started down it, descending through shelves of grave plots like rice patties. Thick fog weaved between old tombstones like the wispy fingers of a thousand ghosts, curling around wooden crosses and whispering softly. I often heard voices, often saw things scurry into underground grave vaults. The fields of the dead were more extensive than I could have imagined. After an unthinkable amount of time, I made it to a plateau, a sort of middle ground between the hilltop crypts and the forest below.

From here the trail branched in two. The way forward descended through the staggered plains of dead and into the spooky forest. The other way went left and climbed up the hill where Jack's bar sat like a haunted hotel, its neon sign flickering behind a screen of fog. In the moonlight I could see for miles along the plateau, more nameless gravestones than a man could count. From them came a ghostly orchestra, thousands of long and drawn-out wails cascading over each other. The sound frightened me. The dark forest below frightened me. I thought about going the shorter way to Jack's place. Maybe the crafty bartender would be resurrected once again, willing to harbor me from the leagues of noisy spirits.

But no. My path was through the woods. I could feel it.

I was about to continue my descent when I spotted something disturbing just off the trail. It looked like carrion, something dead being eaten by ravens. They tugged and yanked with their beaks, swallowed bits of dead flesh. I thought it was an animal. Then I saw the gravesite where it had been dug out of, the soil scattered by the hungry birds. The tombstone had a scrap of paper taped to it, someone's name written in runny red wax. It was the little girl's grave desecrated by the birds. And there she was, long dead and food for scavengers.

"Get away from her," I said, trying to shoo them away. I stepped off the path and into the weeds, thinking to put the girl's body back in her grave. Yet the moment I strayed from the path I felt absent, displaced, totally empty. It was like the light switched off in my head. My spirit was slithering from my body.

I had to retract my foot before I lost myself. It appeared the field of dead was dangerous, that it would erase me if I ventured into it. I tried not to look at the girl's half-consumed corpse as I made my way towards the woods.

I was close, walking through the meadow at the bottom of the massive hill, the rises of graves and crypts and

Trial 23

vaults looming behind me like some sprawling city of the dead. The gravesites were sparser at the bottom, no more than a spattering of broken stones stuck from the earth like broken teeth. Flowers and weeds, small shrubs. And imposing before me, the great wall of timbers and the darkness within.

Then it all changed. The grove warbled like a liquid mirror. The mouth of the forest shimmered and a portal manifested itself in the middle of the path. Through it I saw Mr. Strong's sharp shoulders and his bald head. He was walking through the corridors of Wentworth. As I moved forward, the portal grew wider and I was absorbed into it, found myself walking through the hallway behind Mr. Strong, Mr. Clean's raspy breath at my back.

I didn't freak out. I have become accustomed to the dramatic shift from shadow world to Wentworth's dreary interior. I kept following behind Mr. Strong, feeling that my hair was still wet. We must have just left the showers. "Are we going back to my cell?" I asked.

"Did you have somewhere else to be?" Mr. Strong said. And he laughed, villainous cunt.

They indeed deposited me in my blinding cell. "We'll be seeing you real soon," Mr. Strong said, the hint of something wicked in the way he said it, a hot flash of malice as he closed the door and locked me in my wretched hole. What's the skeevy bastard up to?

Now that I've written it down, I think I did miss something. There was significance in the megalithic graveyard. It surely represented something, perhaps my buried past, perhaps all the people I have forgotten shunned and forsaken to wander as ghosts throughout the lost plains of my mind. And Jack, the sneaky fuck. He makes me wonder—his seedy bar towering above the monuments to the dead makes me wonder—in my life, did I seek salvation at the bottom of a bottle?

Either way, I still can't see the big picture. I'm no closer to finding myself than I was on day one. Plus I'm getting hot again, gentle heat fuming from my pours. I feel like a fucking furnace. Why? It's making me sleepy, even weak. It's only mid-day and I'm exhausted. I'd love to speculate further, scribble for another hour about what hidden meanings may or not be lurking beneath the things I've seen, who I may or may not be, but I'm burning up. I think I'll wash myself with cold water from the sink and lay down.

Trial 23

Boris Chapman's personal log: October 28/10

What a clusterfuck. An absolute fucking clusterfuck. Today was a doozy. First off, Windhelm's boy asked Edgar and I to take him to the showers this morning during breakfast. Fuck it, why not? We took the kid. He was under the spout for three fucking minutes before he started slapping the shower wall. "Let me out!" He screamed. "Someone let me out of here!"

Edgar and I snickered at him, naked and slapping the walls of the shower like a fucking ape. We let his mania run its course, then had him follow us through the halls, the kid plodding along real slow like a zombie. He snapped out of it right before we locked him in his cell.

And that was the fucking normal part of my day!

The afternoon was a mess. We went to get the kid for lunch, the usual routine, and he was fucking naked again! Fucking nude, soaked in water from the sink and walking in place against the wall. Face, chest, pressed against the wall and his legs moving like he wanted to walk through it. When I touched him, the crazy kid screamed and went limp, hit his head on the ground and started to convulse.

Sure, Edgar and I might be murderous bastards with a taste for defiling psychotic ladies and occasionally boys with long hair, but we're not total fucking savages. We picked Windhelm's patient up by his arms and legs and carried him twitching to the medical bay, which is connected conveniently to Doc's lab. Honestly, we couldn't have asked for a better excuse to get near where Windhelm stashes the crazy juice.

It was outright pandemonium from the second we got the kid on the table. Dolores was there, screeching at us to keep his limbs from flailing. The nurse stuck a retainer thing in his mouth, stopped him from chomping his tongue off. "Get the straps, strap him down," she barked. We did. Then Mandalay showed up. I don't know who the fuck told her what was going on, probably Gus on the fucking monitors. But there was Mandalay freaking out. "Where's the medical team," she said. And I thought, what fucking medical team? She was irate. "Someone get Windhelm. Someone get the doctor!"

Dolores went for Windhelm. While she was gone, the kid practically fucking died on the table. He went stiff and cold as a corpse, fell asleep or something, slipped into a coma. I don't know. I'm not a fucking doctor. But he was rigid in an unnatural way, fingers bent in weird directions, jaws locked, limbs stressed and the veins in his neck bulged.

Mandalay was losing it. "Everything's okay, John. You're going to be okay." Stroking the kid's cheek like he was her husband. Why was she so concerned? Haven't her and Windhelm killed like 30 patients here with their testing? What's one more brain-fried idiot to her?

Pretty soon Windhelm showed up. What a boss, huh. Doc strolls into the room in his knit sweater, sleeves rolled up to his elbows, big ol' stogie in his teeth. "What's happened here?" Barking at Mandalay like it was her fault. "How long has he

Trial 23

been tensed?"

I answered him. "About forty minutes."

And Windhelm contemplated, stroked his thick beard and puffed cigar smoke into the room, clouding the medical bay. What a fucking quack. "Dolores," he said to the nurse, "run and fetch me John's journal from his cell. Go, woman. Time is of the essence."

Dolores hoofed it out of there. What the hell did Windhelm want with the boy's journal? He was going to save him by reading his diary? Fucking quack.

But here comes the good part. Doc looked straight at me and said, "Boris, I need you to go into my lab. On the third shelf of the metal rack beside my desk are vials. Blue, yellow, green, and red. I need you to get me a green vial and bring it back here. We may have to shock John out of his premortem rigor mortis before his heart stops. He is stressed to the max. John is going to blow out his veins, tear his own muscles to shreds and cause a cerebral hemorrhage."

I told him, "In a flash, boss." It was fucking perfect.

I went from the room, sneaking Edgar a cocky grin as I slipped out the door. Windhelm's such a dummy. Fire me, huh? Threaten me? Idiot. I found myself alone and unsupervised in his lab. I took the green vial off the shelf, yeah, but I also took the red vials. All of them. I emptied the trash can under Windhelm's desk and filled the bag with nearly fifty red vials. Then I scrounged for his box of pills. I knew he had it in there somewhere, and sure enough I found it in one of his desk drawers. Hundreds, man. Fucking hundreds and hundreds of little white pills. The label on the container read,

Trial 23. I fucking emptied it.

On my way back to the medical bay, I dumped the bag of drugs in one of the trash cans in the hall. Today's Thursday. The cleaners won't come until Monday. If all goes according to plan, they won't come at all. Wentworth will be a pile of ashes by tomorrow morning, scrubbed off the fucking map. At the very least it'll be a goddamn zoo.

Trial 23

<u>October 29th, 2010.</u>

I had been lost for some time, adrift in a dark, dark wood.

I had no memory of entering the forest, nor could I recall how long I had been meandering down the twisted dirt trails with mad demons cackling from the bushes. It felt like a lifetime. I was hollow as I walked along, numb and forlorn, a shade away from death. The grove was grim, hushed, bleached in perpetual twilight, a timeless nightscape, a moonlit limbo without thought.

A great bird circled above the forest canopy, cawing and I saw its monstrous shadow soar overhead like the daunting umbra of my life. The whoosh of its wings, the sense it was searching for me. I hurried along in fear.

I soon came to a fork in the road where a thickly gnarled oak loomed like a depressing totem where the path split, a flock of white-eyed ravens nesting in its leafless branches. The birds squawked as I came near, agitated, flapping their black wings. I yelled at them, "Shut up, I hate you." And they frenzied, flapped and squawked like psychotic chickens until they burst into flames and fell off their branches, hung upside-down from the tree like roasted bird carcasses. Only, they weren't birds anymore. They were charcoaled babies. Dozens of cooked infants hung from the branches by cords wrapped around their tiny ankles.

I ran, took the left path and sprinted until my

lungs burned and I forgot how long I had been running. Still, I could not escape the dead babies. They snapped out of the treetops and swayed by their ankles, bodies crisp and red. I couldn't escape them. I couldn't escape the thousands of beer bottles dangling from branches on strings and clinking together like rustic windchimes.

    The stench of cooked meat. The glass chimes. The faint roar of an engine. The sweeping shadow of the huge bird above and the inhuman shapes following alongside me in the obscurity of the woods beyond the path. I broke down and screamed. I covered my ears and screamed as loud as I could.

I almost lost myself in the woods. It felt like a thousand years that I walked on in sullen misery. Many times I had wanted to quit, lay in the bushes and let the nightstalkers take me. But I persevered, kept on despite my growing exhaustion, and eventually emerged from the gloomy forest.

    I found myself atop a hill. Below me was a cathedral, a glorious sanctuary in the heart of a bleak valley. It was a lonely thing beneath the black-blue sky, beneath the pale moon, nothing but solemn hills behind it.

    I rushed down the slope, arms flailing as I ran towards the church, its bronze bell ringing loudly from the belfry as though to herald my arrival. The gong of the bell awakened me, brought me back from the thoughtless hollow of the woods. When I came to the doors of the steeple I felt alert, aware, ready to go inside and discover what was hidden in such a remote place; a church on the other side of a haunted forest, at the base of a mountain of dead. Surely answers!

    I entered the domain of God, someone's god. The steeple had been prepared for a wedding. White balloons were trapped in the dusty rafters, bouquets of

Trial 23

lilies arranged at the ends of the pews. A happy place, I thought. The church had once been a happy place, perhaps the happiest in all my dream vistas. Yet it had been corrupted and spoiled by time untamed. In the pews were skeletons, spiderwebs in their mouths and eye sockets and webbed between their armpits. I wondered if the wedding had ever commenced, or if the guests had waited until decayed to bones.

The echo of my footsteps followed me deeper into the forgotten church. Moonlight spilled through the windows, clouds of dust suspended in the air. As I neared the podium at the end, the massive organ in the corner started to play. A phantom materialized on the bench, hitting the keys, sound blasting out of the huge brass pipes. The phantom played, *here comes the bride.* And there she came from off stage, the black-haired angel, M-somebody in a white satin dress.

She arrived at the altar and stood with her hands folded, veil up, looking eager to be wed. I could hardly believe how beautiful she was, how much I wanted to storm onto the stage and take her in my arms. She looked down the length of the church with a nervous smile, lips red as blood.

I waved to her. "Hey, it's me. I haven't forgotten you." But she couldn't see me. Her form was ghostly, just an apparition, a stain from the past.

I tried going to her, but something stopped me, an invisible force like a spider's web. I got caught in it, couldn't back up or move forward. I was paralyzed in the center of the aisle as the woman grew despondent, sad, waiting for a husband who wasn't there. She paced for a bit, sat on the edge of the stage and kicked her legs like a bored little girl, but eventually gave up. She hung her head and sighed, took one last glance into the pews of skeletons and walked off stage. Her wedding hadn't come. The organ music stopped, the platform dimmed, and the stage reset.

It was a time-lapse, a scene change. The stage went from dark to dim and under the glow of the center lamp was a short stone pillar. On the pillar was a ceremonial bowl used in the baptisms of children, a crude baptismal font. The woman returned to the stage in a scarlet robe, cradling a naked baby in her arms. She struck me as sullen, in dread of the coming ritual.

Her child squalled and the skeletons in the pews jittered in excitement. Savage dead. The fuckers were drunk, I could see. They had beers, clinked their bottles and poured beer down their meatless necks; howled with laughter, clattered their mandibles psychotically like a choir of crazed marionets. They rioted when the priest appeared on stage. I couldn't believe my eyes, the pale beast from the mirror in Jack's toilet. The bastard wore a black robe and came to loom over the altar like a demon priest, his powdered face and his hot red eyes.

Then the perverse ritual began. The pale beast waved his hands over the baptism bowl and the water turned to flames, a little flaming tub for the woman's infant to be christened in. My breath caught when she handed him her child. I wanted to scream, *how could you give him your baby?* But I couldn't. My lungs constricted. The invisible web squeezed my body into a rigid knot, had my teeth clenched, my fingers flexed unnaturally. I was crippled by toxic paralysis. Only my eyes could move, seeing the hooting skeletons, the phantom wailing on the organ and making the tubes honk violently, and the pale beast as he dipped the naked baby into the fire.

Hard to watch. Impossible to look away. The woman was already crying when the pale beast held up her cooked child by the leg, innocent cherub looking like a roasted turkey. He gave it to her and she cooed to it, rocked the smoldering babe in her arms as she walked

Trial 23

off stage and vanished.

I still couldn't move. I was enraged by what I had seen and so tense I thought my blood vessels would burst and I would bleed internally. The goddamn phantom at the organ was pounding out horrible blasts of noise and the skeletons had passed out drunk and their bones were soaked in beer. And still I was tangled in the invisible web!

The pale beast—monster, roaster of children. He dipped his hands into the bowl of fire and began to toss ribbons of flame about the church, igniting the walls, the pews, the damn rafters with wet clumps of napalm until the place was burning.

It quickly filled with smoke. The roof started to cave, to break apart. The pale beast tore off his robe to reveal his mutated body, ripples of white muscle and slithering green veins, a dusted titan seething as the roof came down around him. Burning beams fell, crashed, and in moments he was consumed by black smoke.

And finally I could move again. I jolted into action, released suddenly from stasis. The way forward was clogged with smoke and debris, rivulets of fire spreading over the hardwood floor. I had to turn tail and run, sprint down the aisle and past the fiery skeletons. I kicked open the front door and fled outside, tripped and scrambled on my hands and knees through the grass, then sat to watch it burn.

The midnight sanctuary was engulfed by an inferno. Its roof caved in and the belfry collapsed, toppled sideways into the pit of combustion and the bell rang one last time in a rush of flame and spark. Then the Earth quaked. A gulf opened and swallowed the wreckage of the church, a loud woof of fire and wood as the whole mess was sucked into a sinkhole.

When all was said and done, I sat at the edge of a hole in the ground, a formidable gateway like the black cavemouth to Hell.

Harold Kish

The Journal of Dr. W. Windhelm. Dated 28th of October, the year 2010.

John's mind has failed him. He descends now into a stark hell I cannot imagine. Like the others who came before him, John threatens to forfeit himself to the nightmare abyss. He has immersed himself completely. He has burrowed into the literal graveyard of his mind. His family, surely, were the ones entombed beside him.

    A waste, really. John had been so close to salvation. The pieces were there for John to see. The map was laid out before him. All John had to do was remember. Even I, just by reading his journal, was able to surmise a detailed version of John's miserable existence before Wentworth, before his accident. It begs the question: Why did John remain ignorant? And why did John allow himself to be consumed by the nightmare?

    The procedure did its part. My science is flawless. Trial 23 gifted John the ability to revisit the most impactful moments of his life, his

Trial 23

most traumatic memories. Yet his lifetime of trauma proved too severe. His damaged psyche twisted the memories unearthed by the procedure, morphed them into chilling playgrounds riddled with demons. If only John had seen beneath the allegory, seen the manifestations for what they really were, perhaps he could have remembered. He could have avoided spiraling all the way to the nightmare's core.

It is too late now. John is deep in the maze. It seems the absolute truth of John's life is so regretful that he will fight against it unto the bitter end. John faced the bastard abuser of hell, the pale beast in the mirror, the eater of fear, and yet the final truth is so sickening his brain will not let him touch it. The great secret is locked inside a monstrosity. In fact, whatever happened to John was so crippling that he entombed himself in the graveyard of his past rather than remember it. His subconscious fears it so intuitively that John chose to ramble amongst the tombstones of every other dead memory than unlock the very worst of them, the cradle of guilt that keeps him bound to the fantasy realm, the very epitome of despair.

At least he rid himself of Jack, the smiling embodiment of John's addiction. It does not take a master's degree in psychology to understand what Jack represented, the elixir he symbolized. And yet John thwarted him, pushed Jack into the void. Now Jack is gone. There is nothing to keep John from the heart of the labyrinth.

It must lay through the dark wood at the bottom of the graveyard. The wood is likely a last wall of defense against the hidden pain at the core of John's amnesia. Jack was the guardian, sent to keep John from remembering whatever terrible truth frightens him so badly. Likely what Jack had done for John in the real world. It is all symbolism. And the bleak forest is the final barrier between John and the heart of his soul's darkness. If John is to awaken from his coma, he must venture deep into the ugly innermost chamber of his heart and face the final dreadful monster there. He must find the source of all his pain and look it straight in its eyes, then accept it. Elsewise, John will never awake. If he does, he will be raving mad. I will have to lock him in the dungeon with the others.

Eight o'clock in the evening and John is still deeply submerged, his eyeballs flickering behind their lids as he lay prone on the table, I am sure. I wish there was a way to see through his mind's eye, to witness the final confrontation between John

Trial 23

and the keeper of his most horrific memory, the root of his nightmare. It must be a truly abhorrent creature.

Alas, there is no way to infiltrate John's brain. I must wait to see if John makes it through his last trial. Perhaps he will write everything down afterwards and I can read it. I would hate not knowing. I am rather invested in his tale. It would be like missing the final chapter of an exciting book.

Margaret remains in the medical ward with John. The woman was a mess throughout the entire day, an emotional wreck. She had tears in her eyes when I jabbed John with the syringe Boris brought me, the green vial from my laboratory. He handed me the vial and I promptly injected John in the neck with it, releasing a powerful mixture of relaxants, sedatives, and hypnotics into John's system. It is a cocktail of sorts, something to make the most crazed patients docile. It worked. John's tension eased and he slipped easily into sleep. Though I was surprised by how hot his skin was, as if he had a rampant fever.

Mandalay was distraught. "What have you done to him, doctor? He's gone too deep. We should pull him out now, wake him up. He is going to be trapped in the dreamworld forever. He is going to go mad!"

"Silence," I told the woman. "John is in a creation of his own making. Only he may find his way out of it. The trial has run its course. John's fate is in his own hands."

"The procedure has done nothing," she said. "Where is the control? Where is the great revelation of John's mind?"

"Unfolding..." I tapped John in the center of his forehead. "In there. John is at the brink of his great revelation."

"I don't understand," she said. "Trial 23 was supposed to give John the ability to control his dreams, to overlap reality with a unique fantasy world. It wasn't supposed to turn him into a zombie."

"I am not surprised," I said. "You are too emotional to understand. You do not see that John already has the ability to control his dreams. It is not my fault his dreams are horrors."

Mandalay gaped at me, looking as John so rightly described, 'like a goldfish.' "Horrors? Doctor, what horrors? His nightmares can kill him. You must know that!"

I was done with Margaret's hysteria. I told her, "I will be in my office if anything changes. Only call for me if John awakens." Then I gave a chuckle. "Or if he dies."

"Boris," I said, the bald goons idling by the door, "Mandalay can handle John. Finish your duties for the day. Take the animals for dinner

Trial 23

at six. Put them in their cages after."

Boris nodded, grinned his sick, hateful grin and left the room with Edgar. I really dislike those two. Maybe I will fire them on Monday.

I left Mandalay to oversee John's condition and returned here to my office. I have no idea how long it will take John to navigate the labyrinth. Time is irrelevant inside the mind. John could wander aimless for what feels like years to him, yet is only minutes in reality. He may already be adrift in the void, lost to forgetfulness. Only time will tell if he finds the strength to overcome.

The hour grows late. Perhaps I will fax some reports to my benefactors, inform them that Trial 23 was a success. It may certainly be used as a weapon of war, a slow-burn of a killer. A mind killer. Because, if I am being honest with myself, the properties of my formula have not had the intended results. True, John created a world within his mind, but he sunk into it. He did not wield it in a creative or beneficial way. He let it consume him. Perhaps Trial 24 will yield more… malleable results.

I should start with someone relatively sane. Perhaps Mandalay. She will not know what I have done until after it is too late, until I have already exposed her to the red mist I have stored in the vials in my lab. I have yet to test the gaseous, more potent version of the procedure. Trial 23 in the white pills took anywhere from twenty to eighty minutes to effect John, depending on his stress level. Trial 24 is a wild card. I will have to monitor the goldfish woman very carefully.

How funny, that my co-creator may become my most valuable lab rat. I only hope for Doctor Mandalay's sake that she is not a cesspool of trauma. How sad it would be for her to end up in the dungeons.

What? The fire alarm has just gone off. There is shouting from down the hall. It sounds like madmen, the screeching of the mad. What the hell is going on? Wait… Someone is banging on my door.

October 29th, 2010.

The pit lay open before me, the black pocket into the Earth. I came to stand at its edge and look in, the way down a mineshaft to the Earth's core. It was red down there, and dark. Something hot bubbled a far way down.

    At the lip of the hole was a sort of dip, like a wheelchair ramp. And that was when I saw the winding path carved along the inside wall of the hole, a gradual spiral into the abyss. The hole itself was immense and the pathway descended at a very slight incline. I stepped down and began the journey, leaving behind the moonlit hills and delving into the hollow.

    I followed the path for a long time, hugging the dirt wall of the pit, going deeper and deeper until I could smell the volcanic stink of sulfur, feel the belches of heat from the red haze below. I had lost the sky, nothing but blackness overhead and the dim glow of the hot core to guide me.

    I was less than halfway to the bottom when the path stopped abruptly. I almost walked straight off the edge. It gave me a good fright, really woke me up. My foot scuffed the edge and I yelped, shuffled back a few steps. Then I saw what I had missed, the archway cut into the soil, a dark corridor leading deeper into the Earth. It was a damn digger's tunnel, utterly lightless. I walked through it blind for what felt like hours, continually sloping downwards, moving deeper and deeper and deeper into a subterranean nightmare.

    The air was getting hot, sticky. My inhalations

were born from a furnace. I felt the heat in my lungs. The ground underfoot was getting hard, becoming rock. It didn't take long before I was creeping through a kind of cave system. Little rivers of magma flowed alongside the path, puddles of liquid fire boiling in shallow craters. There was enough magma to emit a red glow throughout the cave, enough light for me to see by; to see the jagged stalactites on the ceiling, the black spires of stalagmites on the floor; the runny layers of mineral sediment on the wall like melted black wax; the lumps of salt blooming to form crystally toadstools; and the grottos, the pockets of darkness below and above like hide-e-holes for cave goblins.

And it was so hot! Sweltering as I moved through the tunnels. I was slick with sweat. When I stumbled upon the first door, I was so fucking hot I just walked by it, not caring what kind of sordid devil had been locked away in the deepest recess of the Earth. But then I saw more. More and more doors like the ones from the dungeon in Wentworth were embedded in the black walls of the cave. Savage looking things, archaic, banded with iron. A whole legion of bastards had been imprisoned in the fiery belly of the underground. It soon occurred to me that I was in a hive, a complex of tunnels and doors like some secret cave monastery.

I finally stopped to check what was behind one of the doors. I was in an area where magma dripped from the ceiling and the heat was unbearable. The air was cooked. I tried the doorknob and it didn't work. I banged, and from the other side came a gargle of noise like a spastic feral cat.

"Hello?" I said.

Someone crashed into the door and made me jump. "Let me out of here!" She was mad, wailing on the door from the other side. "Please, let me out."

"I can't," I said. "It's locked."

Trial 23

She said, "It's Loise. Please let me out. I beg you, John, free me from this place."

Loise. I thought the name sounded familiar. Hadn't I had an aunt named Loise? And how did she know my name? I thought I was a John doe. It made me wonder, could John be my real name?

"I'm sorry," I said, "I can't help you," and I kept going, the sound of her rattling door following me down the tunnel, her desperate pleas, "Save me, John. Oh god, save me." I was in a damn nuthouse, a special layer of Hell reserved for fucking lunatics, an underground insane asylum!

It took a while, but I figured it out. I had to wander aimless through a series of corridors and passageways for a while, but I figured it out, that I was lost in a maze. The hive of cells was a labyrinth. The tunnels turned sharply left or right, sometimes forked and sometimes I hit a dead end. Always I was disoriented. Always there was a voice screaming from behind a closed door. "It's me, Susan. Don't you remember? Let me out. Don't you dare forget me!"

Susan, yeah. Wasn't she someone's wife?

But not all the doors were closed. Some were left open, the cells inside vacant. There were ugly straw cots and no windows inside, rock walls and a hole to piss in. Miserable cages. All of them miserable.

Then I came upon a chamber unlike the others. This room was large and squared with a squat ceiling and rivers of syrupy magma bleeding down its black rock walls. It was a red dungeon. There were no cells, only one man chained to the wall with heavy manacles around his throat and wrists. I recognized him immediately. Sad fucker with his head hung, his denim jacket dusty and ripped. I'd have been sad too, murdered and my soul torn asunder just to end up in the bowels of the Earth, chained to a wall in a stifling magma chamber.

"Hey," I said, walking into the room. Small magma streams crisscrossed the rocky floor and I had to tread carefully. "I'm sorry about before. I'm sorry about you dying."

He saw me and smiled, his smile full of glee despite his weathered face, his tired eyes. "No worries, man. It wasn't your fault." He stood up, brushed the dust off him and opened his arms, his chains sagging beside him. "Give me a hug, John. Everything's going to be alright, you know."

Fuck it. I hugged him. I felt I had to. And the moment we embraced was when it happened, the goddamn torrent, the flood of memory like a kick to the head. It rocked me and I stumbled back, my hand outstretched as if to keep Joel from touching me. I said, "Joel…"

And he chuckled. "There it is, John. It's about damn time you remember me. A crying fucking shame though, man. You had to come all the way down here to do it. Not sure if you'll make it back upstairs. You've got to get past the beast first, and he's one mean son of a bitch."

I had tears in my eyes. Joel. Jesus Christ it was Joel, my dearly departed friend. "I'm sorry," I said again. I didn't care about any beast. I latched onto him, squeezed Joel as hard as I could. "I left you there that night. I never went to Jack's. I was… I was…"

"I know what you were doing," he said, "and it's alright, man. It's in the past. It wasn't your fault. The guy had a gun. He was rabid, a fucking stunted little monster in a hood. Maybe if you had been there, you'd have got a bullet too."

I opened my mouth to say more, holding Joel by the shoulders and looking in his face, but I had no more to say. I remembered him, remembered the night I had promised to meet him outside of Jack's and never showed, but the rest was blank. I couldn't remember anything other than hearing about his death on the evening news, getting the call from Sharyl. Before, after, between, all blank.

Joel saw my lapse. "It's alright," he said, "the rest will come later. You have deeper to go. The beast is loose in this place. He takes us, you know. He takes people from their cells and no one ever comes back. It's so hot in here, John. I'm so thirsty. I just want to be free."

It was hot. I was roasting in Joel's private hell. The magma dribbled down the walls, bubbled in thin gullies on the floor. I knew I had to keep going, and so did he.

"Go," he said. "She's waiting for you here somewhere. She'll guide you to the center of the maze, to the lair of the beast. Thank you, John. Thank you for remembering me."

"Joel," I said, "I have so much guilt. I don't know what to do."

He only smiled. "Do me a favor, huh, forget about it. See you later, John." And Joel evaporated into thin air. Poof, gone. His shackles clattered to the ground.

I left Joel's chamber feeling like a long-awaited amends had been made. An enormous boulder had been lifted off my shoulders. I felt lighter. Finally, I got to say the goodbye I had been robbed of in life. I had apologized to Joel, and that felt good. But I couldn't ignore the feeling of a greater burden still heavy on my back, a far more detrimental sin in need of atonement. I had to hurry to the center of the maze. I had to collect the rest of my memories!

Leaving Joel's chamber, I entered yet another rock tunnel of locked doors and magma trenches.

People rattled their doors as I hurried by. They were yelling, "John, it's me. Remember Tom? Remember Brandon? Remember Stephanie? Remember Lyle? Let us out!" And yes, I remembered Tom. He was my neighbor. And Brandon, the bald guy from work who ate ham sandwiches every day and always stank like cheese. Stephanie, she was my first serious girlfriend. Lyle, a regular at Jack's place. Yes, I remembered them all. They called out their names and I remembered them!

Then I came to the end of the passage, to the very last door. A man called to me, "Come here, boy. Come take a look at me."

His voice stopped me dead, turned my guts inside out. It was hauntingly familiar. The door of his cell had a barred window and I approached it cautiously, peeped inside and saw an old disheveled man sitting in shadow. His room was dark. No bed, no hole for pissing, just a wasted old fuck sagged in the corner. My father. I recognized the ugly shape of him, haggard piece of shit. An assault of unpleasant memories punched me in the brain and I sneered, squeezed the bars of his cell and grit my teeth. What was the old fool doing here?

He said, "Look at what you've done to me, boy." But he didn't move. He stayed clumped in the corner of his cell, a lump of trash in dark rags, disheveled and bearded.

"Rot," I said, and I moved away from the door. Even frail and beaten as he was, I couldn't stand the sight of him, the putrid stench of his evil. I hoped to God he would rot in that cell for the rest of time. Remembering the face of my father made me sick with hatred, sick with grief. Where the hell was Jack and his sweet bottle of whiskey when I needed him?

Trial 23

Things calmed outside the passage. The heat lessened. There were no more doors. Streams of magma flowed through the uneven rock and guided my way, but they were thinning. The ceiling was low, bony. It was darker here. It felt more like a cave. The air cooled significantly and the way forward dipped. I was fumbling down shelfs of rock. I had to use my hands to descend the rubble, to slip deeper and deeper into the cooling grotto.

I scaled deep. It became difficult to see and I often fumbled for purchase as I climbed down heaps of stone like a fucking spelunker. I sometimes had to squeeze through fissures or get on my belly to crawl beneath an impossibly low ceiling. It didn't feel like a maze anymore. I felt like a worm burrowing into the Earth, a forsaken cave dweller lost in the heart of a mountain.

There was no more heat, no more magma. Water dripped from overhangs and the rocks were sometimes slick. I shimmied between two slabs of stone and found myself in a kind of air pocket, an almost mystical cavern far below the hot prison. It was a tranquil place, sad in a way. The air had a blue tinge to it, the rocks a gentle silver from distant refracted light. It was here that I found my guide. She sat solemn on a rock, all alone in the moody cave like a dreamless pilgrim. Her black hair, dull red lips, lost eyes. She was lovely despite her sadness.

I went to her. "What are you doing in this cold place?"

She was slow to answer. The drip of water filled our stillness and she regarded me with a hollow expression. I could tell she didn't know who I was. Her eyes were fogged. She must have been sitting on that rock for ages. She didn't recognize me, and I still could not remember her name.

"He took her," she said, speaking very slowly.

"He took her below. That was… some time ago."

"Who took her?" I asked. "The beast?"

She nodded, looking half asleep. "Yes, the beast. He has her in the deep below. I have been waiting here for my daughter since…" She trailed off.

I was sad seeing her like that. She had lost her mind, much like I had. We were one in the same, I thought, two hollowed-out people abandoned to a primordial cavity in the Earth. I wanted to help her. I felt that it was my purpose.

"Do you know where the beast is?" I asked. "Can you take me to him?"

Her eyelids fluttered. Something changed, a twinkle of recognition in her sleepy eyes. "You," she said. "You can help me. You can rescue my daughter from the beast."

I made a face, looked deeper into the twilight cavern. "I think that's why I'm here."

"Yes." She was waking up. "Yes, you are here to help me. You're here to save my child. I… I cannot even remember her name."

"Can you remember mine?"

She shook her head. "No, stranger, not even my own."

"But you can take me to his lair, to the heart of the labyrinth?"

She almost smiled, glazed and dreamy. "Yes, stranger. Come, I will show you."

She slid off her rock and floated through the moonglow cavern like a midnight ghost in a shift. I followed behind her. I wanted to talk, to make some simple conversation, but I had no idea what to say. We were connected, I knew, because I felt drawn to her, like she was the second half of my heart. But my goddamn useless brain refused to remember a thing. And she was too much like a ghost, dead without her

Trial 23

daughter.

"What is this place?" I asked. We had walked through the cavern and into a lobby, the main lobby of a hospital. The cave had sort of molded into it. Everything was burnt, the wide desk littered with half burned papers and the computer monitors toasted. The walls had been eaten by fire, ceiling a mess of exposed pipes and wires. At the far end of the lobby was an elevator in perfect condition.

"It's where he took her," she said. "He took her there." Pointing at the elevator. "And he never came back. I sat down on the rock outside and..." She trailed off again.

"And he never came back?"

"No," she said, "never. He's down below."

I remembered what Joel had said about the beast stealing people from their cells upstairs and how they were never seen again. It made me wonder if the woman's daughter was still alive, or if my quest was a lost cause. Was I off to collect the bones of an infant? Perhaps I was meant to be food for the beast. It wouldn't have surprised me if my journey was meant to end in my own pointless sacrifice.

Though none of it mattered. I would have done anything the woman asked. I could not refuse her. She looked at me and I melted, got soft. "Will you go down?" she asked.

I nodded. "Of course I will."

We were at the elevator. "You wait here," I told her. "When I find your daughter, I will take the elevator up to get you, then we will take the elevator to its highest point and try to find a way out of this cruel place."

"Okay." She crossed her arms and stepped back. I didn't dare touch her for fear she would evaporate like Joel had. "Thank you," she said.

I hit the call button for the elevator. There was a

low grumble, pullies and gears switching on and the groan of the elevator being lifted from its depths. A few seconds later came a ding and the doors opened. I stepped inside.

It was a normal elevator, a button for up and a button for down. I pushed the down button and the doors slid shut. I was whisked downwards in the steel box. I never doubted why the woman hadn't gone to get her child herself. I just supposed it was my job, a duty I needed to fulfill if I wished to break free of the nightmare.

The lair of the beast was yet another cave. But it was an ice cave. The air was freezing. I stepped out of the elevator and began through a narrow tunnel of grey rock, shivering as I went. My breath was exhaled in white clouds. I realized I was in the same place the pale beast had been when I saw him through the mirror at Jack's bar. That felt like a lifetime ago.

As I strayed deeper down the icy tunnel, I began to hear a man's voice. "Don't put me in there," he said. "Please don't. Just club me to death. Crush my fucking skull but don't put me in there."

His pleas came crisp in the cold. He was obviously terrified. A few more twists and turns and I made it to the end of the tunnel, where I crouched behind a hunk of stone and gazed stealthily into the lair of the pale beast. Finally, the heart of the maze.

The guy was still begging for his life, or rather for an easy death. "Just let me freeze," he said, cowering against the pocked wall of the cavern. He had on a cheap suit. A lawyer, I thought, the guy's a lawyer. Dave, David? Something like that. "I don't want to go in there," he was saying. "Just let me starve. Cut my fucking head off. Anything but the box."

He surely meant the rectangular box-like contraption in the middle of the domed cavern. It

Trial 23

looked like a fish tank sitting on a stone table. Inside the tank were three sawblades a half inch above its floor. A chute ran from the bottom of the tank to an iron box positioned on a stove burner. From the iron box was a clear plastic tube. It ran from the box to a throne carved from the cold grey rock. Seated in the throne was the pale beast. He sat rigid with his lips pinched, listening to the man (Davis?) beg for reprieve.

"Gouge out my eyes. Kick me in the nuts. Rip my legs off. Just don't put me in the fucking box."

The beast got up, walked around the box and his heavy steps shook the cave. He took the lawyer man and lifted him above his bald white head. Then he threw him in the box.

"No! Oh god no!" The lawyer trying to crawl out of the tank like a dumb lizard.

The pale beast went back to his chair and sat down, pulled a metal lever that jutted from the ground beside him and kicked the box into gear.

A metal roof slid across the top, isolating the poor fucker inside. Then the sawblades kicked on. He didn't even have time to scream before he was shredded. His cheap suit, his skin, his bones and his organs, all shredded into a paste by the sawblades in less than thirty seconds. It was a goddamn blender. The guy's blood splattered the glass walls and the rest of him was reduced to an inch of sludge on the floor of the box.

Then the far end lifted with a hydraulic squeal. The man's gunky leftovers slid down to the chute and were funneled into the smaller iron box. The burner beneath the iron flared orange and began to heat the lawyer's liquid remains. The pale beast sat indifferent on his throne, the thin rubber tube clenched in his ugly teeth. I heard the slop bubbling, turning to gas. The pale one sucked on the tube and a putrid yellow smoke slithered through it. He inhaled it all. In one huge suck, he literally smoked the lawyer man. The white ogre smoked the fucking guy!

    The beast's exhalation was so preposterously enormous that the smoke from his lungs clouded his domed chamber. I could hardly see. The whole room filled with noxious yellow smoke. I crept slowly through it, moving with my back against the wall until I was past the beast and his sick box, to the thin crevice I had seen from my hiding place. I slipped into it, shimmied through the fracture until I came into yet another room.

But not a cave! It was a child's bedroom. The walls were papered baby blue, a kid's wardrobe covered in stickers, a changing table, wicker baskets full of plush animals. It was a cute space. There was even a window with a view of the park outside. A fucking park! Beautiful and sunny, tree branches swaying in a summer's wind. I almost forgot I was stealing a baby from a human smoking ogre.

    My chest tightened when I saw the baby's crib beneath the window. A mobile spun above it, played a happy tune as little fairies dipped and bobbed above the girl's crib. I tiptoed across the room, scared to death there would be no child in the cradle. I held my breath and peeked inside.

    And there she was, adorable and fast asleep, swaddled in a pink blanket. I had to admire her for a minute. She was perfect, little rosy cheeks, no more than six months old. I picked her up and held her delicately to my chest, whispered sweet nothings and felt her soft skin against my face. I wanted to stay there with her forever. I hated that I had take her past the beast and into the caves.

    But the pale beast was out cold. Good thing. The smoke had dissipated by the time I crept into the room with the child tight against my chest. The beast

Trial 23

slumbered in his throne like a fat guy passed out drunk on his recliner. He was blitzed, had no idea I was stealing the child out from under his nose. I hurried around his disgusting contraption and made for the elevator.

She was right where I had left her, the child's mother standing woefully in front of the elevator doors. "Get in," I said, but she just gawked into the elevator, a blank look on her face. She had already forgotten who I was.

Then she saw the baby and her eyes lit up. "You found her," she said. "You found my baby." She hurried into the elevator, took the child from my arms and cradled her, cooed to her, kissed her little red nose. I smiled and hit the up button on the panel.

"He'll come for her," she said, admiring the swaddled girl. "He'll come to take my daughter back. I know he will. He wants her for himself. He wants to keep her in the great below with him."

"Then we better get out of here," I said. "Let's see where this elevator goes."

I watched them discreetly as we went up, mother in love with the little bundle in her arms. Yet I still couldn't remember her name. Had I not completed my mission by reuniting the family? I had thought it was my final test. Why the hell couldn't I remember? I was just as null as before. We slowly ascended in the elevator and I kept thinking, who are you people? What have I missed?

Then we stopped. The doors opened and we were inside one of the black rock tunnels. There was a sudden rush of heat, a great clamor of noise. Someone had let the prisoners out of their cages and they rioted in the tunnel. They fought, screamed, clawed at each other. It was chaos. Twenty maniacs had been let loose in the hall and every one of them turned to stare at us.

"There he is!" Someone shouted. "Make him

remember us!" And the entire horde ran towards the elevator.

"Fuck." I smashed the up button on the panel over and over. The woman cried out, "Get us out of here, John. Get us home!"

Wait, she remembered me?

No time to talk about it. The elevator lurched just as someone who looked a lot like my mailman stuck his arm in and grabbed me. The elevator went up and the dumb son of a bitch got his arm lopped off. The thing flopped around on the floor like a live fish.

We were going up fast. The doors wouldn't shut. An impossibly long shaft hummed by us in a blur while the light inside flickered. The woman hunkered in the corner and protected the infant. I somehow stayed on my feet, the elevator rattling like a damn rocket about to explode. I could hear the bolts coming loose.

Then we crashed.

Trial 23

Boris Chapman's personal log: October 29/10

Windhelm may have been a quack motherfucker, but he was a clever quack motherfucker. He paid a guy to come in and fuck with the air system last year, separate the main building's air supply from the one that feeds the cells. It's a handy thing to have when you're secretly gassing your fucking patients. Well, Edgar and I knew all about it. Bet Doc never thought his clever idea would get him killed.

We did dinner a little differently last night. Not only did we round up the normal nut fucks locked down the hall from Windhelm's boy, but the other ones too. Every last spastic jackoff. We even unlocked the crazy cunts from downstairs and brought them into the cafeteria. There must have been nearly two-hundred crazy shit monkeys packed in there. We had Patty, the lunch bitch, cook them up something real fucking special. Slop. Bowls and bowls of slop. And inside the slop, three little white pills for each of them.

And that was just the start.

Edgar and I watched them eat, snickering, unable to tell which ones had gone off the rails and which ones were already way off the fucking track. It was a bit of a bitch herding them all back into their cells. It took over an hour. The placid fuckers were easy, but the unruly bunch we had to manhandle. The four monsters from below refused to go back and Edgar and I got to bust out the batons we had brought with us, beat the savage fuckers until we got restraints on them. We had to take them down the elevator one by one because they were so fucking feral. Jonas is a spiter, a biter. Doc's pumped Jonas full of more drugs than a back-alley whore. He'll kill just about anything he gets his hands on.

All the trouble was worth it. We successfully drugged every patient in Wentworth with Doc's Trial 23 pills and locked them back in their cells. Then we had to take care of Gus. Doc was so busy with his precious little coma boy; he was bound to keep himself contained to his office until the kid woke up. We took advantage, went into Gus' camera room where he has his wall of monitors, his little fucking eagle's nest that watches over Wentworth.

"What was that all about?" Gus asked. "Why did you bring the beasts up from below?"

"Nunya," I said, and Edgar grabbed Gus and hefted him out of his chair.

Gus was a weasel. He sniveled while we tied him up. "You won't get away with this, whatever you guys are doing."

"Yeah right," I said, and taped his mouth shut. His eyes, too, just for fun. We left Gus cocooned in the corner of his office and went to the furnace room with our bag of red vials.

The process was easy. Windhelm had rigged up a sort of discharge system to the furnace. He also had a complex series of valves installed in the vents to isolate certain rooms. All we had to do was open all the valves to allow maximum air flow to every room, then one by one insert the red vials into the mechanism on the furnace. Windhelm's serum

Trial 23

evaporated on contact with the furnace coils and was absorbed into the hot air, then cycled through Wentworth's 200-odd cells.

Fucking science, huh.

The next part was easy. Wait an hour, let the animals stew in the poison gas, whatever the fuck Windhelm had in those red vials. We hung around and waited in the monitor room, Gus squirming like a worm in the corner. We watched the tvs as the patients got more and more crazy. It was fucking comedy. They screamed at the walls, attacked themselves, fell on the floor and seized. But mostly they were alert, violent and totally fucking deranged. Martin, the old prick, even got a hard on and tried fucking his pillow. Crazy coot.

After letting them suck up a few hundred breaths of the invisible red mist, Edgar and I let the maniacs out. We started at the far end of the hall and worked our way towards the mesh gate, popping the locks quickly and then scuttling away. By the time we reached the gate, heads were emerging from the doors, shouts getting louder as the inmates realized they were free.

We kept the mesh gate locked while we rode the elevator down to the dungeons. We had our batons with us, tasers too in case we had to do some damage. The dungeon doors use old skeleton keys and it's a bitch to unlock them. We got three opened, Edgar working on the fourth when Jonas came bowling out of his cell like a fucking bloodthirsty zombie.

I had to taser him in the face. He didn't fall, just jittered on his feet. "Let's get the fuck out of here man," I said to Edgar. "Fuck Todd. Leave him in there." And I started for the elevator door.

Edgar was right behind me. "I got it," he said

as we piled into the elevator.

    We both looked to see Todd, one of the younger Wentworth patients, a kid with a proclivity for eating human flesh, creep out of his cell and lick his lips. The kid's a fucking cannibal. He's got sharply filed teeth. The hungry look in his eyes nearly made me shit myself as the elevator doors closed. And I'm a fucking convict!

Back in HQ, Gus' fucking eagle's nest, we sat down to enjoy the show. We had the door barred good so the crazies couldn't get in. We had even managed to disconnect the phone lines. Luckily, Wentworth is so far in the fucking bush of Mew's County there is no cell service. No one could call for help. There were three doctors somewhere in the building, including Windhelm, one lunch lady, three more caretakers, and one soon to be very surprised nurse. Nothing left to do but watch the anarchy unfold.

    And what a fucking riot it was! Better than I could have asked for. Though, not so great for Edgar, raping idiot.

    Things got heated pretty quick. It was like watching a hive of busy ants spread throughout the hallways. Maybe it was the mixture of the pills and the gas, but the folks were going berserk. They dragged themselves along the walls, eyes rolling in the backs of their heads. They raved, fucking nuts. They pulled out their hair and some people got naked. There were fights, which were hilarious because most of the crackpots at Wentworth were seniors, 50+. There were a lot of broken hips in the hallways.

    Something about all the chaos got Edgar's blood boiling. "I've always wanted to fuck Margaret,"

Trial 23

he said. "She's so fucking petite, like a little boy with a pigtail and glasses. I'd like to plug up her ass."

I thought, yeah, of course you do, you sick fuck. I let him out and locked the door behind him, watched Edgar troll through the hallways like a big creepy uncle on his way to violate his nephew. At the same time, someone pulled the fire alarm and the hallways blared with noise. Super annoying. I had to disconnect the alarm on the ceiling. When I looked back to the monitors, all hell was breaking loose.

The monsters from below had figured out the elevator and were tearing a warpath through the halls on route, it looked like, to Windhelm's office. Doctor Mandalay was walking through the halls confused, probably about the shrieking and the fire alarm. And there was Edgar, in the middle of everything with a hard-on in his pants.

Mandalay was the only one with any sense. She peeked around a corner and saw the four horsemen of the apocalypse—Jonas and Todd, Franklin and the old serial rapist, Herbert—waltzing down the fucking hallway. She ran from them back into the medical bay. I switched monitors and watched her barricade the door with a desk, then sit beside Windhelm's boy and stroke his hair. Fucking weirdo.

Edgar didn't know Mandalay had fortified herself in the med bay. He made it to her door around the same time the four vengeful dungeon dwellers made it to Windhelm's office. The fuckers were out for blood. Everything happened in a weird, almost divine snap of karma.

Edgar tried the knob. When he realized it was locked, he got mad. I could see it. He was hammering on the med bay door, saliva spitting from his mouth he was yelling so much. On the other monitor, Mandalay cowered by the kid. Her lips moved but I couldn't hear anything. Maybe she was praying. The kid was fast asleep.

Two halls over, the freaks were breaking down Windhelm's door. They had knocked politely, then Jonas had attacked the fucking thing and all four of them made quick work tearing it down. I watched tensely for a full minute. There was no camera in Doc's office. I had to wait until Todd the cannibal came out with one of Windhelm's arms, chewing on it like a stick of corn. I guess they killed him. Shit just got real. Adios, Doc.

Edgar was slowly realizing he couldn't break through the door and rape Mandalay's puckered asshole. Sick fucker. He made do. Mandalay looked to be sobbing inside, and Edgar looked to be listening. He had his ear pressed to the door and his hand in his pants. He was saying something to her, but I couldn't figure out what. She cried, half splayed over the kid's limp body. And on the other side of the door, Edgar with his bare ass to the camera, pumping his dick while he got off to the sound of Mandalay crying.

What a show. And all for free! After Windhelm was torn apart by the wackjobs, I knew Edgar and I would never get away with what we had done. Not with witnesses. Not with death involved. Not with Gus bound in the corner. I had to do something. The psychos were taking over the asylum on the monitors, fueled by Windhelm's psycho drugs. Fuck it, I thought, feed Gus to the animals.

I untied the little wimp and told him, "Go get Windhelm. Tell him what we've done. I've been a

Trial 23

very bad boy."

He blinked at me. "What?"

"Windhelm, idiot!" I kicked him out of the room and barred the door again, then watched Gus struggle through the hallways of deranged fuckholes like a mouse in a maze to Doc's office.

The savages were still in there. Gus had no idea. He figured it out in the threshold. Fuck, I wonder what he saw when he peeked inside. Three brainless goons having a party with Windhelm's organs? Whatever it was, Gus bolted down the hall and they chased him, Jonas half naked and covered in blood. I had lost track of Todd.

Gus—and here comes the divine fucking karma—ended up in the same hallway as Edgar, who was in the process of pulling up his pants and wiping the jizz off his thumb. Gus screamed something, and so did Edgar, and all at once they were under siege by the dungeon fiends, the very worse motherfuckers in Wentworth.

Edgar had left his baton in the room with me. I saw it sitting on the floor and laughed. He managed to taser Herbert in the arm and drop him, but Jonas and Franklin were quick. Edgar's a big fucking boy. He's a mean cunt. But he was no match for pure and brutal insanity. Franklin might have been sixty, wrinkled and hairy, but he had the raw strength of a puma. He jumped, wrapped his legs around Edgar's waist, grabbed his face with both hands, and thumbed out his eyeballs. Edgar opened his mouth to scream, blood squirting Franklin in the mouth and him trying to catch it like a fucking water fountain. Then Edgar was on his back with his eyes gouged out. Jonas kicked his head around until it looked like a crushed melon.

Dumb fucking Gus. He hadn't the sense to run.

He stood trembling like a fool until Franklin and Jonas turned on him, gave him a quick and savage beating. They were a couple of primates, pounded their chests, hooted, clubbed Gus until his face was red and puffed and he was dead. Then Jonas and Franklin went off down the hall, skipping merrily like a couple of schoolgirls.

Herbert recovered from the electrical shock a minute later and sauntered off, probably looking for something to rape.

That was it for me. The anarchy at Wentworth was my hot little potato of an idea. Best to scram before I was implicated. I hadn't imagined three men would be slaughtered, never mind the dozens of old farts I stepped over in the hallway on my way out of the building, either dead or seriously fucked up.

Mandalay was still in the room with Wentworth's boy when I left. As far as she's concerned, the whole catastrophe was Edgar's fault. Lord knows he scared her good enough to start making accusations. I pinned the whole damn thing on him anyway. No one else saw me with the drugs. I stopped at the nearest gas station and made the 911 call. It was a long fucking night after that. Questions, dozens of squad cars, half a dozen ambulances, four firetrucks.

"He was deranged," I told Officer Howie. "Edgar had been talking about it, but I never imagined he would let all those people out. They are dangerous!"

I never mentioned Windhelm's fantasy drugs. I didn't mention his pet project. Let it all die with the doctor. His precious hospital is in ruins. I saw on the news that there was a fire and it burnt down. I

Trial 23
suppose I should start looking for work on Monday.

October 29th, 2010.

The woman and her baby vanished. I don't know what happened to them. The elevator burst through the ground in a loud crash and when I stumbled out of it they were gone. The elevator was empty. It stood in the middle of the road like a misplaced phonebooth. I guessed we had travelled all the way to the surface.

It was night, halfmoon in the sky, crickets chirping in the woods beside the road. I was deep in the country, I knew, some backroad out from the city. There was a bridge very close to me, just up from where the elevator sat crooked in a crater of broken blacktop as though it had fallen from the sky. Beneath the bridge was a lake, black and still. It took me a few seconds of gawking to recognize it for what it was: McGuire Lake

I started walking towards the bridge, and that was when the car came. I heard the roar of the engine, then saw the headlights. Two yellow high beams were cruising straight for me. I was in the middle of the lane and they blinded me. I froze, thinking I was about to be run down by an out of control drunk driver.

But he swerved halfway across the bridge and crashed into the concrete barricade, loud crunch of the hood and a smash of glass as the man was ejected from the driver's seat and sent flying through the windshield. He sailed like a crash test dummy through the air and splashed into the lake below.

Trial 23

I ran to the crash. The car was wrecked, hood bent and smoking, glass everywhere. I hoisted myself over the barricade and looked below, a few bubbles on the surface from where the man had sunk into the lake. I didn't know what to do. Jump in and try to rescue him? It looked cold down there.

Besides, the bubbles were intensifying, something rising quickly to the surface. I had no time to wonder why I was at McGuire lake, why the car looked so familiar. Hadn't something happened here on the West Bridge? I was too concerned with the wet swamp thing rising out of the blackened waters. There was the top of its slimy head slinking towards the shore. I watched it slowly rise, its gross ebony hair veiling its face, decayed flesh and black gauntlets, golden talons, the ornate chest suspended in the hollow of its missing stomach by rotted baby hands. It was the she-beast. She was walking up the embankment, moving around towards the road!

At the same time, a rumble came from below ground. I turned to see the elevator jiggle, be dislodged and a loud roar as the pale beast shoved the elevator out of the hole and emerged from it. He was seething mad, standing in the rumpled pavement and staring at me with his red eyes. He wanted the child back. He wanted the woman's daughter. Where the hell had they gone?

I didn't have any answers for the muscular ape. And the she-beast was nearly at the road. The two ugly monsters saw each other. I was still on the bridge, backed up against the wrecked hood of the car. They were far enough away for now. It was like watching two rival titans meet for the first time. The pale one bawled in anger and raised his huge fists, and the she-beast stared at him with her mask of hair. Then they were fighting.

He started it, charged at her like a fucking bull. I could feel his anger, his hatred of the she-beast. He reached as though to rip the treasure from her stomach, and she caught his wrists in her talons. For all the bulk of him, he was powerless against the amalgamation of dead things. She pushed him backwards, he grunted, and in one hard swing she severed his head with her sharp talons. His huge muscled body flopped to the ground and blood spurted from his mangled neck. His head rolled into the ditch.

    I couldn't believe it. She was a war machine. She had killed every terrifying monster in my nightmares and now we were alone on the West Bridge over McGuire Lake. She lumbered towards me, more imposing than words could tell. But it wasn't just her festering skin and veiled face, the red cloth stitched across her breasts. It was the cursed box in her empty gut. I hated it. She was a freak. I had to get away. I scrambled onto the barricade before she could reach me and dived into the lake.

It was cold and murky. I floated in the middle of a gloomy pool, no up or down, listless like an astronaut in space. Then from the obscurity someone appeared. It was the man from the car crash. He too floated in the stagnant abyss. We came face to face and I saw that it was me. He was me! His features, his hair, his drowned eyes. It was me!

    I tried to swim away, but the floater grabbed hold of me. He was still alive, a gash on his head slowly bleeding into the water like spilt ink. I had to fight against him, against me. He was trying to pull me to the bottom of the lake, strong for a drowned man. I kicked and struggled, and that was when I felt icy claws around my throat. I was being pulled up, the floater slowly fading to the bottom of the lake. How surreal, to watch myself drift into a murky nothing.

    Fucking she-beast. She pulled me from the lake

and dumped me on the rocky shore. I spat out water, coughing on my hands and knees. She was right above me. I had nowhere to run. I'd have rather drowned than confront her.

I got up, trapped between McGuire Lake and the sad truth currently floating to its bottom, and an even more horrendous secret contained in the bowels of the she-beast. I knew it was dreadful. I didn't want to face it. A powerful instinct in my gut told me slit my own throat, bash my own face inwards with a rock or at least gouge out my eyes. Anything but look. *Don't!* It screamed, the faint voice of Jack. *Don't watch, friend! Save yourself!*

Too late. She was folding over herself, bending over backwards into the shape of a table. The ornately carved treasure chest was wobbly in her core, the gross little baby hands. I saw it had a lid and knew what she wanted. She was presenting the box to me. She wanted me to open it. I had to fight against my instincts just to touch it. My bones stiffened, heart cold, hands shaking as I caressed the atrocious thing with the tips of my fingers. Very slowly, I slid open the box.

It was a baby, my baby, Monica's baby. She lay squirming on the red felt underlay of the box. Innocent, adorable, the love of my life. I had been hiding from this all along, since the very beginning? I had run from my own child? Memories of her came flooding back in a torrent of happiness. Her birth, our days in the park, Monica's smiling face at our daughter's baptism. Oh god, I missed my child. I scooped her from the box, lay her in my forearms. "My baby," I said. "I love you, child."

Then she screamed.

"No," I said, "hush. Hush, sweetness." But she kept wailing as if in terrible agony. Her skin got hot, so hot it burned my forearms. Something awful was happening. A memory broiled in my head, flashes of fire, an apartment building engulfed in flames. My little girl was breaking apart in my arms. Her skin was bubbling in yellow sores, burnt patches searing her flesh. There was nothing I could do. I held her as she fried. Her hair crisped and fell out and her scalp went red and cracked. Her squalling stopped and her face pinched, sucked in, tiny eyeballs melted to white jelly that slid back into her skull. It didn't stop until my daughter was a thin layer of cooked meat overtop brittle bones, so small I held her smoking corpse in my hands.

    I dropped to my knees and screamed. It was the sort of scream from a night terror, screaming and screaming and I just wanted to wake up.

Trial 23

Margaret's Journal: 10/30/10

I'm not sure where to start. Wentworth is shut down. I spent the last two days speaking to police, to detectives, to lawyers. It's been a nightmare. I had to fight through a swarm of press to get to my car at the police station. They were shouting, "What happened at Wentworth? Did you witness the bloodbath? Was Doctor Windhelm involved in malpractice? Did you have anything to do with it?"

So many questions. They hurdled them at me relentlessly. I wanted to scream, "Yes, it was me! Windhelm and I killed them! We've been subjecting innocent people to radical drug trials for years! I burned down the hospital to cover it up! There's a pile of ashes in the basement, more than thirty people!" But I didn't. "No comment," I said, and rushed through them to my car and drove home.

Only now am I getting a chance to write down what happened. It spiraled so quickly. One minute I had been preparing to oust Windhelm and his trials and steal John from the hospital. The next, John was comatose in the medical bay. And then... Oh Jesus, and then Edgar was trying to break down the door. "Let me feel your coochie, you little bitch," he screamed at me. I just cried. It was so scary. I think I'm traumatized for life.

There was a struggle in the hallway shortly after. Edgar screamed, and I thought I heard Gus' voice. It lasted just a minute. There were sick sounds, gushy like someone splattering fruit in the hall. I heard laughing, then it was over. The fire alarm continued to blare in the hallway but that was it. I huddled next to John for the better part of the next two hours until he woke up screaming.

John jolted awake from what I suspected was a very bad nightmare. He continued to scream even when awake. His eyeballs were huge and he thrashed on the table. I had forgotten John was strapped down. I quickly undid his restraints. He sat up, tears flowing down his cheeks, poor boy in complete disarray.

"What happened?" I asked.

John said nothing. He broke down and cried. He sat on the table with his face in his hands and cried for a very long time. There was a deeply emotional pain in his sobs. His heart was broken. John wept and wept until he had nothing left. Then he sat on the table and stared dully across the room. After a while he said, "I want to go home."

"Home? John, do you remember where home is?"

"Yeah." He didn't sound happy about it. "67 Brookwood Drive. East Side."

"Oh my god, John. Your memories, are they back?"

"Yeah." He still didn't sound happy. He stared straight ahead like he was staring into the past.

"Well, what do you remember?"

Unlike John, I was very excited. I was astounded our formula had worked. We had actually managed to heal John's amnesia. I had a thousand questions for him. I wanted to ask John what had happened to him in his dream world. I wanted to know what he was feeling. I wondered if John could do everything Windhelm had promised now that his memories were back. It was very exciting, very scientifically intriguing. I wanted to put him

Trial 23

under immediate observation. I wanted to scan his brain while he slept. I wanted to probe him. I wanted to give John a new series of trials to test the limits of his healed mind. I couldn't believe it. The possibilities were suddenly real. Mind manipulation and creative freedom at its most potent!

Also, I wanted to fetch Windhelm and give him the good news. With John safe, I was feeling a lot better about our tests.

But John was sulky, sad about whatever he had uncovered. "I remember everything," he said. "I want to go home now, Margaret. I'm done."

Then I remembered what was going on in the hall, the four terrorizers from the dungeon loose somewhere in the building. "Uhm, John, there's been an incident. I think Edgar let out the patients. I saw them screaming in the hallways. Edgar tried to break in here, but something happened. He might be dead outside the door."

John screwed up his face. "Too much death," he said. "I need to get the fuck out of here. I don't care." He got off the table and moved to the door, paused to listen. "I don't hear anything now."

He was right. The fire alarm had stopped and there were no more sounds of commotion from outside. "It's not safe," I said. "We should wait for the police."

John shook his head. "I'm going home, Margaret. I don't know what kind of bullshit you fucking doctors did to me, but I remember what happened now. I wasn't thrown from a taxicab. I drove myself into the fucking river. Windhelm lied to me. He made me think I was insane. He put me through a series of terrible hallucinations and kept me locked in a cell like a fucking lab rat. I'm done, Margaret. I'm out of here."

I didn't know what to do. John had every right to be angry. He was an unwitting test subject. An experiment, really. And he knew it. I could see the anger in his eyes; and something more, some horrible grief tearing him apart.

As John opened the door I said, "Wait, let me drive you." And I went with him into the hall.

Sure enough, Edgar had been murdered. The ugly man's head was concaved and his eyeballs had been pushed into his skull. He looked like a scrambled egg. Served him right for trying to violate me. John stepped over his body and I followed, careful not to step in the blood. Gus was there too. Poor little Gus beaten to death. I hoped the murderer had gone away.

I took John down the hall, finding more evidence of the chaos that had been unleashed in the hospital. Kicked in doors, smashed lights, muddy footprints. Where the heck had they gotten mud? And where the heck had they all gone?

"Wait," I said, "I need to check something."

John waited while I scampered quickly down the hall to Windhelm's office. I shrieked when I stepped inside and found the doctor laying in a pool of blood with his arm missing and a hole in his stomach, blood splashed around the room like finger-paint. Someone had torn Windhelm apart!

John heard me scream and came running. "Fuck," he said, looking in at Windhelm's horribly desecrated corpse. John seemed more surprised than upset. Understandable, given the circumstances. But I was aghast. I had expected to find the doctor smoking a cigar behind his desk. I had intended to tell him I was leaving with John and that he had dead people in the hall, and that he should hide whatever needed hiding. It was too late for that. Windhelm had been picked apart by his own patients. A sort of karma, I guess. But he had been an amazing psychologist, a truly brilliant scientist. A touch insane, but brilliant. It was sad to see him ended in

Trial 23

terrible violence. Though maybe he deserved it. Lord knows Windhelm caused a lot of suffering over the years.

"I just need to get something," I told John. I had my satchel with me, the one with all the details of our trials, 1 through 25, as well as the information on our departed subjects. I went to Windhelm's desk and took anything that looked important, including his journal. That was how I found out later what he had planned to do with me. I guess I was lucky. Now that I think about it, probably a good thing he was killed. Windhelm had plotted to betray me and lock me in a cell!

Windhelm's shinny Zippo lighter was on his desk and I used it to light some loose papers on fire.

John asked, "What are you doing?" And I told him, "It's best for everyone if this information dies with the doctor." Then John nodded. I supposed he agreed.

He came over to join me at Windhelm's desk. John's journal was laying on a stack of books and he picked it up right before it caught flame. "I want to keep this," he said. I didn't argue. I didn't ask what for. After I started a fire on the floor beside Windhelm's bookshelf, we left the room.

Martin was dead and naked in the hallway. Poor old man. A few of the older residents were in terrible shape on the floor. It looked like they had been fighting, much of their faces bruised and discolored. And yet they didn't look to be in much pain. Their eyes shined strangely. They appeared lost in private hallucinations, the elderly patients like drug addicts moaning to themselves as they lay against the walls of the corridor. It was haunting.

We got to the front door and I realized very suddenly where all the patients had gone, and why the hospital was so quiet. They had escaped, walked right out the front door and wandered off into the night. There were maybe 200 unstable psychotics moseying around Mew's County.

I wonder how many they've caught, if Todd and Herbert, Franklin and Jonas, are out there terrorizing the nearby farmers. It's a scary thought. Sad too, thinking of all the delirious patients lost and afraid. Wentworth is gone now. What will the state do with all those people? I hope the police find them and put them somewhere safe.

We got in my car and left the parking lot, started down the long drive to the county road. Looking in the windshield, I marveled at how daunting Wentworth was at night, a big mausoleum of sorts, a kind of haunted mansion in the middle of nowhere. It felt good to be leaving. Sad though, that our work had finally made progress only for Windhelm to die, the patients to escape and the hospital to be condemned. I saw the fire already raging in the windows of Windhelm's office.

John didn't say much. "Aren't you happy?" I asked. "You snapped out of your amnesia. You can finally go home."

"I don't want to talk about it," he said.

Something about John bothered me. I couldn't understand why he wasn't happy. Sure, we may have abused his trust a little bit. We might have drugged him just a smidge. But he was all better. He was going home. Why did he sit in the passenger seat and sulk like a baby?

"Do you want me to stop calling you John?" I asked. "Did you remember your real name?"

He laughed hysterically. He laughed so hard it caught me off guard and scared me. At the same time, I saw people rustling through the bushes beside the road, nightstalkers prowling the highway. It was the escaped patients! And then came the sirens. Police cars raced in the direction of the hospital. Squad cars and ambulances. Even a fire truck. The red and blue lights illuminated the interior of my car and John looked more insane than I had ever seen him. He howled mad with laughter in the passenger seat. "It is my name," he said. "That's the fucking kicker. My name is John. My fucking name is John."

Needless to say, it was a very uncomfortable car ride. Adrenaline had kept me from freaking out in the hospital, but once John and I were on the freeway I had a mental breakdown. I had to stop the car at a gas station to cry for five minutes. I was a nervous wreck. Maybe it was the tears, but I could have sworn I saw Boris eating a cheeseburger while talking to a police officer inside the little diner beside the gas station. I swore it was Boris.

The rest of the drive was even more awkward. Neither of us said much. I wanted to counsel John, but I was so nervous. My throat was dry. My hands were numb from squeezing the steering wheel. Even when we entered the city, John only spoke to give directions. He was so haunted. I wanted to help. All I could do was wave goodbye and wish him luck when I dropped him off in front of the place he said was his house.

Not much of a house. I was concerned watching John go up the walkway, holding his journal to his chest like a kid with his schoolbook. The grass was overgrown, windows dark, two months' worth of mail sloppy on the doorstep. It was clearly neglected. Though, I supposed John hadn't been home in a while. I waited for him to go inside before driving away.

That was yesterday. Today I'm out of the job, but I've talked to my lawyers and they think we can draft a pretty substantial lawsuit against Windhelm's estate. He was worth a fortune. He owned the hospital and a few other properties. My lawyers think I'll be able to sue and seize control over most of Windhelm's assets. Maybe I'll build another hospital. I still have the notes, the formulas, the information on the amnesiac patients. Jesus, not to mention the information I have on the dozens of other experiments. Maybe I'll check up on

Harold Kish

John in a few weeks, see how he's holding up. Trial 23 should forever have altered his brain waves. He should have the ability to manipulate hallucinations at will. He might never leave his house again.

Trial 23

<u>October 29th, 2010.</u>

We moved into this house with the insurance money from the fire. Who'd of thought years of buying into home insurance would pay off. "Psychological damage," they called it, "emotional duress." Yeah, no shit. We liked the house because it had no memories. It was a blank slate for Monica and me to start over. The walls were eggshell white, unblemished hardwood floors, pristine showers that had never been used. We had to buy all new stuff, but it was a good distraction. It helped to rebuild piece by piece. Until all the pieces were in place. After that it was just empty. Horribly and vacuously empty.

    So I drove into the lake. Well, I hit the barricade and launched into the lake through the windshield. I don't remember clearly. I was drunk. The car wasn't even mine and I didn't have my wallet, probably why no one could identify me at the hospital. Although what really happened was that I smashed through the windshield of the car and landed in cell 244, Wentworth Psychiatric Hospital. What happened next is logged in this journal.

    I guess I'm writing the last chapter of my crazy nightmare-dream-hallucination-delusion-fantasy-shadow realm-drug coma-fuck town-hippy bullshit as… what? Catharsis? Maybe I'm trying to purge myself of my shitty life and my shitty time at Wentworth before I go upstairs to join Monica. She's up there waiting for me. She's been waiting a long time. A few more minutes to finish my extraordinary tale won't make much difference. Maybe someone will turn it into a book.

    I've got to hand it to Windhelm. The fucker's dead now, but he did a swell job piecing my brain back together. Lack of oxygen, if I had to guess. I had been underwater for too long before I washed up on shore. My brain got wet, memories washed right out of my head. Cut and dry, you ask me. But Windhelm, he did a swell job with whatever drugs he gave me. In my food, in my water, in my damn air. I have no idea. All I know is they worked. Even after Mandalay dropped me off at home last night, I still found myself plugged into the dreamscape.

    Mandalay was sweet. She was very concerned for me, trying to talk to me during the car ride. Though I suspect she just felt guilty for whatever her and the good doctor had done to me. It didn't matter. I refused to speak. All I wanted was to get home to Monica and cry my soul out for what a bastard I am. It's true. I'm a real repugnant son of a bitch, a real destroyer of worlds. I said goodbye to Mandalay and got out of her car, walked to my front door. It was unlocked. I turned the knob and went inside.

The foyer was much as I remembered it, but dirty and cluttered. There was a peculiar film in the air like a dead mist. I went into the kitchen, dirt dishes piled in the sink, on the counters, moldy vegetables in the refrigerator. The place was a dump.

    "Monica," I called, but no one answered. The air was getting thicker, a dusty haze of thin ash.

    I went to the backdoor and looked outside. The yard was overgrown with weeds. An enormous raven sat in the middle of the tangled lawn and groomed itself like a prehistoric vulture. It made me think of my sister.

Trial 23

I went for the staircase thinking to check the upstairs bedrooms for Monica. Maybe she was having a nap. Or maybe she was at work. The air shimmered fiercely as I climbed the stairs, heavy with static. I hit the landing and it was like walking through a mist of golden flakes, tiny flecks of gold twinkling in the air. At the end of the hall was our bedroom. It was a big house for only two people. I moved through the golden fog. "Monica, are you there?" And went into our room.

It was mostly the same. Everything was right where it ought to be. Our queen-sized bed was in the middle of the room, Monica's shoe trunk at the foot of the bed, her big vanity on the left side of the room cluttered with makeup paraphernalia, my closet on the right with my dusty clothes hung up on hooks. But the back wall was missing. The back of the room was an open portal, an otherworldly gateway to a heavenly plain. Beyond the bed was a round platform, a megalithic set of golden stairs leading towards a brilliant city in the clouds, tall sparkling towers and winding spires, everything gold, everything shining. It was the Kingdom of Heaven in all its magnificent glory. I was standing at the threshold of eternity.

And there was Monica, my lovely wife hovering above our bed. She was beautiful with her angel wings, her fans of pure white feathers. They were the source of the mist, flapping softly and shedding golden flakes like dandruff. "John," she said to me, and even her voice was angelic, "you've come home at last."

Monica's halo glowed bright yellow, her eyes an impossible shade of blue. And her garb, her extravagant robes of white and silver and gold. I had never seen her so radiant. I wanted to embrace her, yet I feared my touch would burn away her wings.

"Monica," I said, "I'm so sorry. Can you ever forgive me for what I did? I can't live with the guilt. It tears me apart inside. It scratches day and night at the corners of my mind. My heart is in tatters. All I see when I close my eyes is our innocent little angel engulfed in flame. I need release, Monica. I need deliverance."

"Yes, John." Monica smiled and opened her arms. "Come to me, John. Let us seek eternity together."

I was afraid. How could I embrace an angel when I was such an abhorrent devil, such a godless worm? I reached very cautiously for Monica's outstretched hand. Our fingers touched, my skin prickled, and the portal behind Monica warbled and the image of a distant heaven went dark, black. "It is not for us," she said sadly. And I knew something was wrong when her smile faded. "You are damned, John. You are damned and you've damned me."

I reeled back, Monica's wings burst into flames as she screamed, "You've damned me, John. You've damned me!" Fire consumed her wings and her halo slipped down her face and around her neck like a collar. It pulsed bright yellow and constricted, strangled Monica and her wings turned to ash and sprinkled the bed. The room was dark but for her glowing halo. It kept her suspended in the air. It was choking my wife! Her face went red, then blue. Her arms twitched by her side. She sputtered, bit her tongue and blood soaked her chin. She was in horrible pain, her legs flailing a foot above the mattress. Then the light of Monica's halo faded. My wife hung by a dull band around her throat, dead and limp above the bed.

That was two hours ago. I've been writing downstairs at the kitchen table since then. I'm not sure why. It just feels important that I complete my journal, wrap up my story from beginning to end. Wentworth was a nightmare, but it was a hell of a lot better than

Trial 23

remembering. A part of me wishes Windhelm had kept me locked in the lower dungeons after I killed the old man, Bernie. It had made a suitable perdition. It had fit the crime. But if I concentrate hard enough...

Yes, there we go. I've morphed the kitchen into the dungeon cell. Now I'm sitting at my table in the dank and grimy confines of the medieval chamber. Look, there's my piss pot in the corner.

Hold on, let me focus...

I'm in the kitchen of our old apartment now, sitting in the corner of the room and watching Monica spoon-feed our daughter mushy green baby food. Monica's laughing. The girl's squirming in her highchair. It's such a nice memory. I think I'll stay here a just a little while longer. Why live in a nightmare if I don't have to?

Harold Kish

The End

Made in the USA
Middletown, DE
17 May 2021